] hidden tale

Bello is a digital-only imprint of Pan Macmillan,
established to breathe new life into previously published,
classic books.

At Bello we believe in the timeless power of the imagination,
of a good story, narrative and entertainment, and we want to
use digital technology to ensure that many more readers
can enjoy these books into the future.

We publish in ebook and print-on-demand formats
to bring these wonderful books to new audiences.

www.panmacmillan.co.uk/bello

B E L L O

Margaret Dickinson

Born in Gainsborough, Lincolnshire, Margaret Dickinson moved to the coast at the age of seven and so began her love for the sea and the Lincolnshire landscape.

Her ambition to be a writer began early and she had her first novel published at the age of twenty-seven. This was followed by twenty-seven further titles including *Plough the Furrow*, *Sow the Seed* and *Reap the Harvest*, which make up her Lincolnshire Fleethaven trilogy.

Many of her novels are set in the heart of her home county, but in *Tangled Threads* and *Twisted Strands* the stories include not only Lincolnshire but also the framework knitting and lace industries of Nottingham.

Her 2012 and 2013 novels, *Jenny's War* and *The Clippie Girls*, were both top twenty bestsellers and her 2014 novel, *Fairfield Hall*, went to number nine on the *Sunday Times* bestseller list.

Margaret Dickinson

BELOVED ENEMY

BELL

First published in 1984 by Robert Hale

This edition published 2014 by Bello
an imprint of Pan Macmillan, a division of Macmillan Publishers Limited
Pan Macmillan, 20 New Wharf Road, London N1 9RR
Basingstoke and Oxford
Associated companies throughout the world

www.panmacmillan.co.uk/bello

ISBN 978-1-4472-29016-2 EPUB
ISBN 978-1-4472-29014-8 HB
ISBN 978-1-4472-29015-5 PB

Visit www.panmacmillan.com to read more about all our books
and to buy them. You will also find features, author interviews and
news of any author events, and you can sign up for e-newsletters
so that you're always first to hear about our new releases.

Author's Note

My writing career falls into two 'eras'. I had my first novel published at the age of twenty-five, and between 1968 and 1984 I had a total of nine novels published by Robert Hale Ltd. These were a mixture of light, historical romance, an action-suspense and one thriller, originally published under a pseudonym. Because of family commitments I then had a seven-year gap, but began writing again in the early nineties. Then occurred that little piece of luck that we all need at some time in our lives: I found a wonderful agent, Darley Anderson, and on his advice began to write saga fiction; stories with a strong woman as the main character and with a vivid and realistic background as the setting. Darley found me a happy home with Pan Macmillan, for whom I have now written twenty-one novels since 1994. Older, and with a maturity those seven 'fallow' years brought me, I recognize that I am now writing with greater depth and daring.

But I am by no means ashamed of those early works: they have been my early learning curve – and I am still learning! Originally, the first nine novels were published in hardback and subsequently in Large Print, but have never previously been issued in paperback or, of course, in ebook. So, I am thrilled that Macmillan, under their Bello imprint, has decided to reissue all nine titles.

Beloved Enemy, published in 1984, is a light, historical romance and was the last book published during the first 'era' of my writing career.

Chapter One

'Now, Charmian my love,' said her mother, tucking a stray golden curl beneath the child's close-fitting bonnet and smoothing down the pale blue gown. 'You promise to be a good girl and not to disgrace your father?'

The 10 year-old girl regarded her mother solemnly. 'Where are we going, Madam?'

Her mother sighed. 'To visit your father's half-sister and her family at Gartree Castle. You—you are to be betrothed to your cousin, Joshua.' There was a catch in her voice.

A small frown creased Charmian's brow; her candid blue eyes were fixed upon her mother's face. 'Betrothed? You mean I am to marry my cousin one day?'

Elizabeth Radley nodded, her lips trembling so that she could not trust herself to speak.

'But—but I don't even know him,' Charmian paused and then said, with a child's directness, 'What if I don't even like him?'

Tears sprang to her gentle mother's eyes and she touched the girl's cheek with shaking fingers. 'Oh my dear child, how can I tell you? It is your father's wish you should marry his half-sister's son. Having no sons of his own . . .' Her voice faltered and Charmian knew her mother was thinking of her own two infant sons who lay in the family grave. 'He—he wishes to unite our family even more closely. Come.' Elizabeth Radley took hold of her small daughter's hand. 'It is time we were leaving.'

Charmian looked down at herself again—at the new gown she was wearing. She could not remember ever having worn anything so fine before. It was fashioned in pale blue silk, the bodice decorated with tiny pearls. On her feet were dainty blue satin slippers, and now around her shoulders was a darker blue velvet cape. She glanced too at her mother.

'I've never seen you look so pretty, Madam.' She reached out her fingers to touch the gown her mother wore. Its bodice was tight with a low, square neckline and the flowing skirt was divided in the front to show the under-petticoat decorated with embroidery and pretty ribbons. Her mother's fair hair, normally hidden beneath the plain, close-fitting white bonnet of a Puritan wife, was dressed in loose ringlets with soft tiny curls on her forehead and thicker curls against her pale cheeks. Entwined in her hair was a string of pearls. But Charmian's compliment, instead of bringing a smile to Elizabeth Radley's lips, only seemed to make her more anxious.

As they descended the stairs together to join her father, Charmian felt her mother's hand tighten on hers almost to the point when the child wanted to cry out in pain.

Joseph Radley turned impatiently. 'Ah, there you are, come along, come along, 'tis time we were . . .'

Then he stopped and stood quite still, his expression darkening as he watched them come down the last few steps and stand meekly before him.

'What is the meaning of this?' His voice was an angry whisper. 'How dare you dress yourself—and the child—in such an outrageous and unseemly manner?' His hand gestured towards the low-cut neckline of his wife's new gown.

'It's her b-betrothal. I thought—it would be a celebration and . . .'

'A celebration!' The word was a blasphemy to Joseph Radley. 'The sober, solemn pledging of two young people. Not an occasion, I assure you, Wife, to indulge in such—such ungodliness.'

Elizabeth Radley winced and Charmian felt her mother begin to shake.

'Return upstairs immediately—those gowns are to be burned. Do you hear me, Wife? *Burned*, I say!'

His bellow of rage followed them as, almost running, Elizabeth Radley dragged her daughter up the stairs once more.

Back in the bedchamber, Charmian watched helplessly as the tears ran down her mother's face. Silently she helped her mother to disrobe and put on the plain black dress with its high neckline and white collar and cuffs. Then she too slipped out of the lovely silk gown and put on her own grey dress. The few moments of happiness, of joy in wearing such pretty clothes, were gone. Even the blue cape was whisked away and the grey mantle she usually wore took its place.

In a strict Puritan household such as that of Joseph Radley, no finery was permitted. Elizabeth Radley, before her marriage a beautiful, joyful girl, who had delighted in lovely gowns and luxurious garments, had made the mistake of wanting the same thing for her daughter. She would not be forgiven, she knew.

During the journey from Boston to the Masons' castle home in the Lincolnshire Wolds, the atmosphere in the coach was uncomfortable. Joseph Radley was still angry and his wife sat next to Charmian with downcast eyes. The child sighed and took to gazing out of the coach. It was a clear, sharp day in September and already the leaves were golden and tumbling to the ground. Such wonderful bright colours, Charmian thought, the greens and browns and golden colours. If Nature were allowed such vibrant tones why then was it so wrong for her to dress in pretty clothes? But her 10-year-old mind could not answer her own question. She felt only the unfairness of her father's strict ruling. She stole a glance at him.

Joseph Radley sat opposite seeming to occupy the whole seat himself. He was a short, stocky man, and grossly overweight for his height. He wore loose-fitting breeches, a jerkin and doublet all in sombre black with the broad white collar and the tall steeple-crowned hat of the zealous Puritan man. His hair was close-cropped and his clean-shaven face was round and florid and grew purple when he was in a rage. It was still showing signs of that very colour even now, some time after his outburst of anger.

Joseph Radley thought himself an important man. Not only was he a successful cloth merchant, but an alderman of the town of Boston. Even more importantly he was an ardent Puritan—an independent like his mentor Oliver Cromwell. The independents wanted to decentralize the Church and put the power in the hands of each individual congregation. Joseph Radley sought power. He had found a measure as an alderman, but he sought more. In Cromwell's shadow—a shadow which Joseph Radley was convinced would grow and spread until it covered the whole of England—he believed he could achieve that ambition.

For the last six years, ever since King Charles had raised his Royal Standard at Nottingham in August 1642, England had been in a state of civil war. As an alderman, Joseph Radley had been one of the main leaders in declaring Boston for the Parliamentarians. The ebb and flow of the revolutionary cause had had its effect on the town. At times they had found themselves almost cut off by Royalist victories. Then as the Parliamentary army moved northwards, Boston was once again linked to Puritan strongholds. Joseph Radley soon managed to get himself noticed by the Parliamentary leaders by sending provisions to the troops of horse to assist the Puritan cause.

The war had dragged on, swaying this way and that and the Parliamentary forces used that time well to organize themselves. An army of the eastern counties under the Earl of Manchester was formed, and Oliver Cromwell was appointed as lieutenant-general of horse. Boston became a kind of refuge for the Parliamentary commanders where they would meet to hold their Councils of War. Joseph Radley made sure that his house was ever open to such men who needed a night's rest and food.

Charmian—throughout her growing years—and her mother were ordered to keep to their apartment though, once, from the top of the staircase Charmian witnessed the arrival of a small, squat figure, with piercing eyes, whom she later learnt to be Oliver Cromwell.

By January 1644 the differing beliefs and desires of the leaders within the Parliamentary cause had exploded. Joseph Radley had returned to Boston from attending the House of Commons in London in a state of high excitement.

'We must support Cromwell, he is the man to lead us to victory. Neither Manchester nor Willoughby have the strength, the power, the vision to see the Royalists crushed . . .' As he had spoken he had pounded his fist into the palm of his other hand.

From that moment Joseph Radley had singled out Cromwell as the man with destiny in his grasp and he had devoted himself to Cromwell's cause. Now, at this moment as they approached Gartree Castle, Joseph Radley was sitting in the coach congratulating himself on his foresight. At Cromwell's side, he had the chance to become a man of even greater power, of the highest position even. Already he was a ruling voice in the government of the town. He meant to purge Boston of any Royalist voice, of any being who spoke against the independent belief. In time, together, they would rid the towns, the counties, the country, of any such voice.

As Joseph Radley saw the towers of Gartree Castle ahead he smiled, feeling satisfied with his world and his future.

The coach jolted over the rough tracks, throwing the silent occupants this way and that, so that by the time they were passing through the guardhouse and over the bridge across the moat and into the enclosed courtyard of Gartree Castle, Charmian felt her small body to be battered and bruised.

The castle stood at the far end of the courtyard from where their coach had crossed the bridge. It was a square building in dark stone and the southern wall fell sheer into the moat. The castle towered four floors high, topped by a defensive parapet and with four guard towers protecting each corner.

The courtyard was alive with activity; low buildings, which housed the soldiers of the castle, ran around the edge of the yard against the high wall and on the eastern side a small footbridge led across the moat to the castle's gardens and then down to a river which half-encircled the whole castle area, providing even more fortification.

As the coach drew to a halt in front of the northern side of the great building, Charmian stepped down shakily as a manservant opened one of the three doors leading into the castle.

'My dear Joseph!' A small stout woman, in Puritan dress similar to their own, was hurrying forward her hands outstretched towards Joseph Radley.

'My dear sister.' Charmian's father was greeting the woman. 'I trust we find you in good health? And your family?'

'You do indeed, Brother. So this is my niece?'

The child was obliged to submit to the woman's severe scrutiny. Looking up at her aunt was like looking at a feminine form of her father, so alike were the half-brother and sister.

Joseph Radley was the son of Abraham Radley and his first wife, Ruth. She had died five years after Joseph's birth. His father had married again and Mary Radley Mason was the child of that second union, some ten years her half-brother's junior. Nevertheless, their resemblance to each other was strong, and not only in physical appearance. Mary Mason, too, was an independent and a devout follower of Oliver Cromwell.

Charmian noticed that Mary Mason and Elizabeth Radley greeted each other politely but coldly. Even the plain Puritan dress could not hide Elizabeth's beauty and, beside her, Mary Mason appeared even to the child to be old and ugly though she knew her mother and her aunt to be the same age. Instinctively Charmian drew closer to her mother as together they climbed the worn stone steps and entered the fortress-like home of the Masons.

The household, Charmian found, was run in much the same manner as their own. If anything, it was even more lacking in comfort and any kind of luxury than their house in Boston. The vast stone rooms were cold and often unheated. The autumnal evenings and early mornings found Charmian and her mother shivering. The furniture was sparse and, such as there was, was heavy and uncomfortable. Even her mother was expected to sit on a stool whilst Joseph Radley took the oak armchair. For Charmian, there was no seat at all.

'We shall hold a small ceremony tomorrow evening,' Mary Mason informed them, 'when the betrothal will take place. It will be a simple, solemn occasion, Brother, as is our custom.'

Joseph Radley nodded agreement and he glanced towards his wife, remembering, no doubt, her vain attempt to bring an air of celebration to the occasion. Mary Mason, it seemed, could do no wrong in her brother's eyes, Charmian thought ruefully, whereas her poor, gentle mother could do nothing right.

Charmian did not meet her uncle nor her future husband until the next day. When she did meet them, she was surprised at the marked difference between her uncle, Edward Mason, and her own father. She had thought all men would be like her father—stern and powerful and somewhat rough in his ways. She did not look to her father for affection or gentleness and therefore did not expect to find it in any man. Her father was a being to be respected perhaps, but mainly to be feared and obeyed.

Edward Mason was a thin man, slightly taller than her father, with gentle, rather frightened eyes, soft hands and a quiet, mild voice. But Joshua Mason—the son—resembled his mother, his rotund shape accentuated by his short cropped hair. He wore a black Puritan suit and white collar. The boy had obviously suffered from rickets—a common disease amongst children—for his legs were cruelly bowed, a deformity not helped by his obesity.

'Spoiled, if you were to ask me, in spite of all their fanatical Puritan ways!' Charmian had overheard her mother's maid mutter. 'His mother dotes on him.' Her words had been addressed not to Charmian but to her father's manservant. So often their servants voiced opinions in front of the child, forgetting that with every passing year the once uncomprehending child now began to understand some of their conversation.

'This is your cousin, Daughter. Shake hands now,' her father ordered, whilst her aunt looked on critically.

Charmian tried to smile and held out her hand to the boy who was some four years her senior. Joshua Mason took her hand reluctantly, pumped it up and down with a vicious tug and, out of view of his elders, grimaced at her. Immediately Charmian retaliated by sticking out her tongue at the boy, but she had not taken the precaution—as he had—of committing the act unseen. Immediately her father raised his hand and struck her on the side of the face.

'You deserve a beating, girl,' he bellowed with rage. 'Go to your room this instant.'

Charmian left the gathering in disgrace, her cheek smarting. Behind her Joshua grinned with smug delight.

That evening she was again called down to the grand hall. The family were waiting for her at the far end of the room and Charmian, a tiny, lonely figure in her grey dress and white apron, was obliged to walk the full length of the hall all the while feeling their unforgiving eyes upon her. Only her mother smiled at her tremulously, but even she glanced towards Joshua Radley to be sure he had not seen the loving gesture.

Charmian stood meekly before her father.

'You will go down on your knees and beg forgiveness from Joshua and from your aunt and uncle,' her father shouted, his face purple. The vein in his temple throbbed—a sure sign of his extreme displeasure.

In a moment of stubborn defiance, Charmian hesitated. Slowly, threateningly Joseph Radley raised his hand.

'Charmian, please,' came her mother's terrified whisper from behind her.

Charmian knelt on the cold stone slabs. 'I beg your forgiveness Aunt Mason—Uncle.'

'And now your cousin,' her father roared.

There was a silence whilst Charmian fought with her inner feelings. Again her father drew back his hand but at that moment the two doors at the end of the main hall were thrown open as if a whirlwind had entered the castle. A huge man strode into the room. He was tall and broad, his cloak flowing behind him. He had an up-turned moustache and a small, pointed beard. His hair curled down to his shoulders. His clothes were of silk and brightly coloured, and the broad-brimmed felt hat he carried in his hand was decorated with three white floating plumes.

'Aha, a family gathering, I see. Why were we not invited, Brother-in-law?' the huge man laughingly addressed Edward Mason, his booming voice echoing round the hall. Edward Mason coughed and shifted uneasily from one foot to the other. All eyes turned to the stranger, Charmian's misdemeanour forgotten. She saw her father's hand fall to his side and risked a glance at his face. If anything, the stranger's arrival was causing her father to grow even more angry than had her playful prank.

The newcomer returned briefly to the doorway and shouted, 'Come in, come in, I was right, you see. 'Tis a family gathering. And,' he turned back towards the Masons and the Radleys who were still standing in a stunned group, 'are we not family?' Again he was striding towards them, his hands outstretched towards Charmian's mother, Elizabeth Radley.

'My dear Elizabeth, after all these years!' He took her mother's trembling fingers in his own huge hand and raised them to his lips. 'As beautiful as ever.'

Charmian looked up at her mother. She was pale and yet two bright spots of colour burned in her cheeks.

At that moment two more people appeared in the doorway.

'Come along, Georgina,' the man boomed, 'don't you want to see your brother, Edward?'

A small, slight woman came hesitantly into the hall and seemed to sidle towards Edward Mason who greeted her with quiet affection, though he was obviously still very ill at ease and kept casting anxious, furtive glances towards his own wife.

Charmian's eyes found the third stranger—a young man of about 18 or so, she judged. A handsome young man, almost as tall as his father, with the same laughing eyes and generous mouth and dressed in the same flamboyant style.

'Well, well, well. And what is all this about, eh?' the older man was saying in his resonant voice.

Mary Mason said stiffly, 'Exactly! What are you doing in my house, Sir Geoffrey Denholm? I do not remember requesting your company?'

'Oh—_your_ house is it now. Mistress Mason? I do not recall being banned from Gartree Castle when I paid court to your husband's sister.'

'Times have changed, sir. I'll have no—_Cavalier_ under my roof.' She almost spat out the words.

At that moment, the stranger seemed to become aware of their mode of dress.

'Good God—you're not followers of that damned Cromwell! No—no, b'God, it cannot be.' His gaze came to rest upon the bowed head of Elizabeth Radley. 'It cannot be,' he murmured softly.

'I'll thank you not to vilify his name in my house,' Mary Mason snapped.

'Nor in my presence,' Joseph Radley said stoutly, standing beside his half-sister. But Sir Geoffrey did not appear to be listening to them. His gaze, filled with a kind of sadness, was fastened upon the lovely face of Charmian's mother.

Chapter Two

After the arrival of Sir Geoffrey Denholm and his wife and son, the proceedings, for Charmian, seemed to pass by in a blur. She was conscious only of the big man's commanding presence, of his booming voice, his ready laughter. But it was perhaps his son, Campbell, who really captivated the 10-year-old girl. Lady Denholm was a quiet, docile creature, like her brother, Edward Mason, and together they seemed to merge into the background and almost disappear.

At the ceremony of the betrothal Charmian found herself standing beside her moody cousin, Joshua, but her eyes sought the face of Campbell Denholm standing near his father, watching her, his laughing mouth unusually grim, his brown eyes sober and mysterious.

After the ceremony—meaningless to the girl-child—there was a plain meal to which Mary Mason was obliged with great reluctance to invite the Denholm family. Puritans lived an austere life. They shunned any form of merry-making, believing it to be sinful. The only form of entertainment they were allowed was music, but even that had to be of a solemn nature. The food spread out on the table followed this belief for it was wholesome yet simple and unextravagant. There was a vegetable soup followed by venison, beef and chicken and then fruit pie and custard and ale to drink even for Charmian and Joshua.

Seated at the table beside her future husband, Charmian was disgusted by the boy's eating habits. It seemed he could not stuff the food into his mouth quickly enough. She watched as he chewed upon a chicken leg, the grease running down his chin. Then across the table her eyes met Campbell's gaze and, with a child's artlessness, she smiled at him. If only, she thought, Campbell were my betrothed instead of Joshua.

Amongst the adults, there was a distinct atmosphere of discord and tension. The arrival of the Denholm family had been an embarrassment to Mary Mason and Joseph Radley, but because Lady Denholm was Edward Mason's sister, they were obliged to suffer the continued presence of their Royalist enemies and even to sit at table with them. Joseph Radley's hostile gaze, his eyes bulging with ill-suppressed anger, continually darted from the faces of the King's followers to his own wife, Elizabeth. Though nervous of her husband's wrath, nevertheless she seemed to have about her an unaccustomed aura of excitement. There was a brightness to her eyes and a faint smile upon her lips which Charmian noticed but could not begin to understand. And Joseph Radley's face never lost its purple hue during the whole evening.

'When does the music and dancing commence, Mistress Mason?' boomed Sir Geoffrey.

'Dancing?' Mary Mason's face was scandalized. 'There'll be no dancing *here*, sir!'

'A pity,' remarked the Royalist drily and his eyes twinkled roguishly. 'I doubt your young daughter has ever experienced the pleasures of the dance, eh Radley?' He rose from his chair and held out his hand towards Charmian. 'Come, my pretty princess, I shall teach you.'

Joseph Radley was on his feet in an instant, thumping the table with his fist. 'I'll thank you, sir, not to introduce my daughter to your evil ways!'

The amusement fled from Sir Geoffrey's face. 'You insult me, Radley.'

'Ay,' the other growled, leaning over the table towards him, whilst Charmian watched with interest, her glance flitting backwards and forwards from one face to the other. At her side, oblivious to everything else, Joshua carried on eating.

'I'll insult you right enough, *Sir* Geoffrey!' Sarcasm lined his salutation. ' 'Tis a mystery to me why you are still at large. Your King is our prisoner now and Cromwell will take power yet.'

'We're not finished yet awhile, Radley. Whilst His Majesty lives . . .'

'Ha—*whilst* he lives,' Joseph Radley mocked. 'He thought he was being very clever, did he not, escaping from Hampton Court and fleeing to the Isle of Wight?' He laughed derisively. 'But what did he find when he got there? The Governor was a Parliamentarian!'

Sir Geoffrey's jaw hardened and, Charmian noticed, his son rose quietly from his seat and came to stand at his father's side.

'You may seek to kill the King,' Campbell said softly, 'but you will never succeed in killing the monarchy. King Charles and his heirs rule by divine right . . .'

His words were drowned by Joseph Radley's roar as he shook his fist in the faces of the two loyal King's men, outnumbered in this Puritan household. But to Charmian's young eyes it was the commanding presence of the flamboyant Sir Geoffrey and his handsome son which filled the room and outshone all the rest of the company.

Edward Mason was on his feet now too trying to make himself heard. 'Please—please! This is a family gathering. Please let us forget for one evening at least our differences.'

Gradually the tumult subsided and the guests sat down and resumed their meal, but the vein throbbed purple in Joseph Radley's temple and his fists lay clenched upon the table.

In spite of everything, Sir Geoffrey was determined to stay at Gartree Castle and the following afternoon, whilst Charmian was walking in the grounds with her mother, he and Campbell suddenly appeared beside them.

'Elizabeth, I must talk with you,' she heard Sir Geoffrey say to her mother in a low, urgent tone. 'Come, down near the river there is an arbour where we can talk undisturbed and unseen from the castle. Campbell can show the little princess the swans.'

'No, Geoffrey, I cannot—I dare not!' her mother began, reluctantly, but Charmian cried eagerly, 'Oh, yes, please,' and gave a squeal of delight when Campbell swung her high in the air, seated her on his shoulder and galloped down the slope out of sight of the windows and towards the river. Charmian's merry laughter ran out in the September air. Watching their antics, even Elizabeth Radley's face lost some of its lines of tension.

At the river bank, Campbell stopped and made as if to tip Charmian headlong into the water. She screamed in genuine terror as she felt herself slip from his shoulder, but as she fell forward she felt his strong arms about her and he was laughing down into her face. Her demure white cotton bonnet was dislodged and fell off and her golden curls tumbled down her back.

For a moment Campbell's eyes were solemn, then swiftly he was laughing again. 'My beautiful Princess Golden Hair,' he said and gently touched one of the fine silken locks.

'You haven't shown me the swans yet,' Charmian said.

Campbell set her down upon the ground and then took her hand. 'This way, Princess, to the swans.'

'Wait. What about my mother, I . . .'

'Oh, your mother can see you.'

'But I must tell her.' Charmian made as if to pull away from him but his grasp tightened upon her hand. 'No.' His tone was sharp. Charmian followed his glance towards the arbour and saw her mother seated there with Sir Geoffrey. The handsome Royalist was holding her mother's hand between his own two huge hands, as if trying to warm life into her. He was leaning towards her talking earnestly, and, as Charmian watched he raised Elizabeth's hand to his lips and kissed it gently, almost reverently.

'Come, we must not disturb them. They have many years to catch up on.'

'What do you mean?' asked the innocent child.

Campbell looked down at her and said gently, 'My father and your mother knew each other many years ago.'

'Oh. Were they friends?'

A small smile quirked the corner of his mouth and the wryness in his tone was lost upon the child. 'I believe they were very good friends, Princess. Look, here are the swans.'

'How lovely they are. So white and see how they glide in the water.' Charmian clasped her hands in sheer delight. 'Oh look, look, there are some young ones swimming behind their mother. Do look, Campbell.'

'I'm looking, Princess,' he said softly. But his eyes were not upon the stately birds but on the excited, animated young girl beside him, her golden curls flying, her blue eyes dancing and her skin aglow in the sharp air.

Presently, her interest in the swans faded. It was then that she noticed a swing tucked up into the boughs of a tree overhanging the path beside the river.

'Do you think I might have a swing?' she asked Campbell with a quaint sedateness that brought a tender smile to the lips of the young man. 'I expect it belongs to Joshua. Do you think he would mind?'

'Why should he? You are his betrothed,' Campbell replied. The smile faded from his mouth and there was a bitter edge to his tone.

'Ye-es,' Charmian said slowly. 'But he does not seem to like me all the same.'

'Do—do you like him?' Campbell asked the girl softly.

Charmian wrinkled her nose. 'No,' she answered with honesty, and added impulsively, 'I wish it were you I had become betrothed to, Campbell.'

'Yes,' the young man replied quite seriously, 'so do I.' But the last words were spoken so quietly and Charmian was now intent upon the swing that she did not really hear him.

Campbell climbed the tree with agility. 'Stand out of the way, Princess, whilst I drop it down.'

'Push higher, Campbell, higher,' Charmian was shrieking with delight moments later, whilst laughingly he pushed once more and then sank to the ground pretending exhaustion.

Charmian giggled helplessly.

At that moment someone shouted her name and the joy and colour fled from her face. Her eyes grew wide with fear. Charmian slipped from the swing, almost guiltily, and Campbell stood up to see Joseph Radley striding down the grass slope towards them. With a gasp, Charmian glanced towards the arbour. Elizabeth Radley, hearing her husband's voice, had jumped to her feet and made as if to run from the arbour which at present obscured her from his view, but Sir Geoffrey put out his arm to restrain her.

Charmian, with only one thought in her head, that of protecting her mother from her father's wrath, ran up the slope to meet him, her hair flying, her skirts lifted almost to her knees, but, breathless, she managed to reach him before he should draw level with the arbour and catch sight of her mother there with the man he considered his enemy. Not quite understanding why, even so the child knew how angry her father would be if he were to see them together. Campbell, obviously fearing the same thing, had followed her towards Joseph Radley.

'What is the meaning of this?'

Charmian faced her father's rage with a beating heart, more fearful of what he should discover in the arbour than of his annoyance at herself for being improperly dressed, with flying hair and rumpled skirts.

'Where is your mother?'

'I—I do not know,' Charmian faltered. It was the first time she could ever remember having told her father a deliberate lie.

'Return to the house immediately and make ready to leave. I have no wish to stay here with these—these Cavaliers!' He glanced towards Campbell Denholm standing a few feet away. There was a sneer upon Joseph Radley's face as his glance ran over the young man from head to foot, over his fine clothes, his long curling brown hair.

'You're a fool, young man, to ally yourself to a losing cause. The King can hold out no longer against Cromwell's Model Army and when the time comes we shall show no mercy to the damned Royalists. Only the protection of your relationship to my brother-in-law has saved you from capture this very day.'

Campbell's expression hardened. 'I grant you the King may not be perfect, but he is the rightful Monarch. Whilst he lives we cannot be overrun by a ruthless dictator who will be followed by many who lust only for power—'

His words struck home and Joseph Radley gave a humourless

bark of laughter. You young pup! What do you know of such matters? You blindly follow your sire . . .'

'No!' Campbell's face, too, was now dark with anger. 'You insult me, sir. I follow the dictates of my own reasoning. Whatever my father is, or does, makes no matter to me. I am my own man and I choose my own path.'

''Twill be a stony one, when we take power.' Joseph's voice was gleeful with menace. You're a fool! Come, throw your hand in with us and I'll see you are rewarded.'

Campbell's anger overflowed and he made to draw the sword at his side. 'Sir, you are offensive to me . . .'

'Now, now, my boy. 'Twill serve no purpose to run this Puritan through. I fear there are still too many left to take his place.' The deep voice of Campbell's father spoke from behind them. Charmian turned to look for her mother, but there was no sign of her, only Sir Geoffrey stood there. 'Our day will come again, Radley,' he added softly, and though Joseph Radley laughed derisively, the Royalist merely nodded. 'Oh yes, our day *will* come, I promise you.'

'Never! The King is beaten. He will have to stand trial and you and all your like will follow him to the block.' He shook his fist towards Sir Geoffrey whilst Charmian watched, shocked by the venom in her father's voice.

Then swiftly, angered by Sir Geoffrey's calm and smiling face, Joseph Radley turned back towards his daughter and raised his hand as if to strike her. 'Are you still here? Back to the castle, I told you.'

She felt rather than saw Campbell make a sudden movement as if to protect her, but Charmian herself dodged the blow as it fell and began to run towards the towering walls of the castle.

The three men watched the swiftly running figure of the child.

'That's a remarkable daughter you have there, Joseph Radley,' Sir Geoffrey said softly. 'One day you may lose her through your own stupidity.'

Joseph Radley's only answer was a low growl of rage.

They left Gartree Castle within the hour. As Joseph Radley climbed into the coach after his wife and daughter, Charmian heard him say, 'You will not forget, Sister, in half an hour.'

'You may rest assured, Brother. It will be just as we have arranged.'

Charmian glanced up at her mother, but she seemed just as mystified by the strange conversation as the child.

'Drive on,' roared Joseph Radley and sat back in the seat, a small smile twisting his mouth. In his eyes there was the glint of excitement. The look sent a shiver down Charmian's back and she was filled with a feeling that something was about to happen. Something that, although it would obviously bring her father pleasure, was most likely to cause distress to her mother and to herself.

She did not have to wait very long to find out. Two miles along the road, her father ordered the coach to pull off the main highway and turn down a narrow cart-track coming to stand beneath the shadows of a copse.

'Joseph—why have we stopped?' There was alarm and fear in Elizabeth Radley's eyes.

'Hold your tongue, Wife,' he snapped and levered his bulk out of the seat and down from the coach. As he moved away Charmian knelt on the seat and peered out.

'Madam,' she whispered. 'There are soldiers all around us. Soldiers from the castle.'

'What?' Elizabeth looked and saw and then sank back into her seat, her cheeks deathly pale, her eyes closed. 'Oh no—no! They m-must mean to ambush them.'

'Who? What do you mean?'

Elizabeth's eyes fluttered open. 'Hush, my dear, you must keep very quiet. We can only hope and pray . . .'

'Madam,' Charmian took her mother's cold hands in hers. 'Please tell me that I may understand.'

Elizabeth hesitated and then haltingly, she tried to explain. 'I believe—your father may have arranged with his sister to lay in wait for the Denholms. No doubt Mary Mason will demand that they now leave her home and—and . . .'

'Oh Madam! Sir Geoffrey and his lady and Campbell—oh no, not Campbell. He has been so kind to me.'

Tears welled in Elizabeth's eyes. 'There is nothing we can do. We are as much—prisoners, as their King.'

They waited a long time in the cold, huddled in their cloaks inside the coach. Outside the soldiers moved about and then suddenly there was a flurry of activity as a runner brought word. The soldiers crouched down on either side of the main highway, their pistols at the ready, at the very moment when Charmian's sharp ears caught the sound of another coach rattling towards them. Not wanting to watch and yet quite unable to tear her terrified gaze away, the child watched as nearer and nearer came the luxurious coach of the Royalist family.

'No—no—*no!*' Her cry of terror was lost amidst the shouts and cries of the soldiers as they leapt from their hiding-places and swarmed around the coach. Pistol shots cracked and the driver toppled from his seat clutching his shoulder. The horses reared in panic, and the coach swayed and rocked dangerously.

'What is happening? I dare not look,' came Elizabeth's whisper.

'They—they have captured Sir Geoffrey. He is getting down from the coach and there is Lady Denholm and—and Campbell. Oh!' The child cried out. 'The soliders are pointing their pistols at them. Oh Madam—they mean to kill them!'

Elizabeth gave a little cry and covered her face with shaking hands. Mesmerized, Charmian was compelled to watch.

'My father is standing before Sir Geoffrey. Oh!' The child winced as if she herself had felt the blow as her father struck Sir Geoffrey's face once, twice, thrice. And then with a mixture of anguish and yet relief she watched the Royalist prisoners being bound.

'They—they are not to be killed,' she breathed.

'Not at this moment, maybe,' Elizabeth murmured hopelessly, 'but what is to become of them? What *is* to become of them?'

Charmian scrambled down suddenly. 'My father is coming back.'

Demurely they waited, trying desperately to appear as if they had witnessed nothing of the drama going on but a few yards from their coach. The door was wrenched open and Joseph Radley heaved himself inside once more.

'The Royalist cause is crushed,' he shouted triumphantly. 'With the King our prisoner and most of his followers in irons or fled the country, there is nothing more they can do. And now—I have the one man who might yet have incited more followers to arms. I have him. I have him! Cromwell will be well pleased with this day's work.'

Silently, Elizabeth Radley bowed her head, her only comfort the small hand of her daughter which held hers so tightly under the cover of her cloak.

Chapter Three

It seemed her father was right after all. The King was the prisoner of the Parliamentarians. He stood trial and was beheaded outside the Palace of Whitehall on 30 January 1649.

Cromwell and his men, her father among them, now ruled England. The growing child heard of these events from the snippets of conversation between the adults around her.

'What will have happened to Sir Geoffrey and his son?' she asked her mother repeatedly in the early years, but Elizabeth Radley could only shake her head and say sadly, 'I don't know, child. I really don't know.'

Unwittingly, it was her father who at last gave her the news she sought—over two and a half years after Charles had been beheaded.

Charmian was sitting on the window-seat in the bay window with her mother, learning a new tapestry stitch, when Joseph Radley returned home. He had been away in London for three weeks. He seemed vastly pleased with himself and he marched up and down the long room, strutting like a proud peacock, rubbing his fat hands together.

'Well, Wife, after all this time I think we have finally crushed the Royalists.' He watched with smug satisfaction as Elizabeth Radley's face paled.

'Charles II—as his Royalist supporters insist on calling him—was crowned King in Scotland and marched at the head of an army of Scots, but Cromwell met them at Worcester and defeated them. Charles got away—to France, we believe.'

He paused, but Elizabeth would not be drawn into asking the question he knew she wished to voice.

'I shall urge Cromwell to dissolve Parliament now and take power himself. I am to become a General in the New Model Army. It was suggested by Cromwell himself for my services,' he added proudly.

'I am very pleased for you,' his wife replied dutifully, but her tone was flat and emotionless and her head remained bowed over her embroidery, though Charmian noticed that the fingers which pushed the needle in and out of her tapestry trembled slightly.

' 'Tis indeed an honour.' He paused and then came to stand close beside Elizabeth. 'I have news of your Cavalier friends.'

Elizabeth's fingers trembled visibly, but she did not lift her head, nor speak. Charmian, however, dropped her work and looked up at her father. 'Sir Geoffrey Denholm, you mean, and his son?'

Her father rounded on her. 'What do you know of it, eh?'

Colour suffused the girl's face. 'Oh nothing—nothing—but . . .' Wildly she searched for some plausible excuse for her hasty question. 'They are the only Royalists we know, are they not?'

Her father gave a grunt and turned away from her, back towards his wife, standing over her, gloating, Charmian thought resentfully. He enjoys making her unhappy.

There was a tense silence while Joseph Radley savoured the drama of the statement he was about to make. 'They were prisoners in the Tower. They have been there these last two years. But they escaped—damned if we know how—and are believed to have gone into exile—with their young King, most likely.'

Elizabeth Radley jumped as she pricked her finger with the needle. Again Charmian could not contain her curiosity. 'But I thought the King was dead?'

Joseph Radley's satisfaction at delivering this piece of news, at seeing his wife's face turn pale and her lips tremble, seemed to mellow his temper. 'My dear child,' he addressed his daughter, though there was not a shred of affection in his words. Never did Joseph Radley use his daughter's given name. It had been the only time he had ever given way to his wife's pleas that their daughter be given a pretty, frivolous name. He had weakened that once, but never in all the years of the child's growing had he ever used her name.

'My dear child, the Royalists believe they are never *without* a King! As soon as one is—disposed of, his heir immediately becomes King. In their view, Charles's son is already the lawful King of England.'

'And is he?'

The vein in her father's temple began to throb. Gone was his brief moment of good humour. 'You should know better than to ask such a foolish question. England is a commonwealth. It became so when we abolished the monarchy and the House of Lords after Charles's execution. England will never again have a king—not whilst I live and breathe!' He turned and strode from the room.

There was silence after he had gone. Charmian raised her troubled eyes to look at her mother, who was sucking the finger she had pricked. Her own eyes mirrored Charmian's concern.

'What—will happen to them? To Sir Geoffrey and—and to Campbell?'

'As long as they stay abroad—away from England—I think they will be safe,' Elizabeth murmured, her voice shaking.

'But what if they should come back to their home and their lands?'

'I suppose their lands will already have been taken over by the Parliamentarians. No doubt Cromwell has given them to one of his men.'

'You—you mean someone else will be living in Campbell's home? Using all their possessions?'

'Or destroying them,' her mother said bitterly.

Charmian was silent for a moment, trying to understand what was happening all around her.

'But what if they should try to come back to save their home? What would happen?' The child, on the threshold of her womanhood, persisted.

A shudder ran through Elizabeth's slim body. 'It would be to certain death whilst Cromwell is so strong.'

Vividly, Charmian could picture the kind of death King Charles had suffered. He had been beheaded, she knew. She could visualize the figure bending over the block, the hooded executioner raising his axe, the swift blow. She swallowed the fear which rose in her throat, for in her imagination it was not the head of Charles, King of England, which fell but the laughing, handsome face of Campbell Denholm.

The years of Charmian's childhood passed in comparative calm. Her father was absent from their home on the outskirts of the harbour town of Boston much of the time on Cromwell's business. At these times there was peace and tranquility in their home, at least on the surface. But Charmian knew her mother was deeply troubled and though Charmian could not ask her the reason outright, her intuition told her that it had to do with the exiled Royalists and the fact that England was in the grip of the puritanical Parliamentarians.

In 1653 Cromwell, though he refused the Crown, was appointed Lord Protector of England, Scotland and Ireland and though there were several plots and uprisings against his rule, these were soon quelled by force by men like Joseph Radley who rose to be one of the Lord Protector's closest colleagues.

But as time went on the rule of the sword and the musket began to become unpopular with the ordinary folk of the land. Fear and hatred of Cromwell and his associates grew and festered as he closed all theatres and banned any form of merry-making. People looked back with affection to the easy-going days under their pleasure-loving King Charles.

By the year Charmian reached her eighteenth birthday, the childhood memory of her betrothal to her cousin had been so blurred by the passage of time that the only strong memory was of Sir Geoffrey and his son, Campbell. The lovely child—Princess Golden Hair, as Campbell had named her—had grown into a beautiful young woman. She knew herself to be betrothed to her cousin, Joshua Mason, and she also knew the Royalists to be in exile and yet her shadowy memory of Joshua had been obliterated—for they had not met again since their betrothal—by her vivid recollection of Campbell who had made such a lasting impression upon the girl-child. The two images had become fused in her mind and in her heart and the only picture she could recall was the face of Campbell Denholm.

The marriage between Joshua and Charmian had been planned to take place when Charmian reached the age of 18.

Preparations were being made at the home of the Radleys for the ceremony when word came that Joshua was ill, very ill, and he lingered betwixt life and death for several weeks. At first it was feared his illness was the dreaded plague. During the years since Cromwell had finally taken power, Mary Mason had opened her house to soldiers of Cromwell's Army as they marched through the countryside quelling any sign of revolt and crushing disobedience of the Puritans' new laws. But with them they brought the risk of all manner of infection. As the days passed after the onset of Joshua's illness, it became apparent that the disease was typhoid—just as dangerous to life and yet it did not bring the certainty of death that plague did.

Word came at last that Joshua had begun to recover, but that because his complete return to health would be slow, Mary Mason suggested that the marriage should be postponed. Her son, she wrote to her half-brother, was not strong enough to make any kind of journey and would need his mother's care for many more weeks.

Joseph Radley was not pleased. His one wish was to see his sinfully beautiful daughter safely married to his half-sister's son and shut away in Gartree Castle. Of course he blamed his wife for the fact that Charmian was becoming difficult to handle.

'You've put fancy notions into her head,' he would storm. 'She seeks pleasure, to be amused all the time. She wishes to dress herself in frippery and has no devotion to her religion.'

'To *your* religion, Joseph,' Elizabeth replied rashly without stopping to think what she was saying.

The vein in his temple throbbed purple. 'Have you sown the seeds of sin in her mind?'

'No, of c-course not,' Elizabeth faltered, heartily regretting her brief moment of rebellion. 'I have tried to teach her your beliefs, but . . .'

'But she has Royalist blood in her—*your* blood! Tainted blood! Oh don't deny it, Wife,' he wagged his finger in her face. Your family—the Parkhavens—would be Royalist if there were any of them still alive but you to *be* a Royalist. And,' he added, his lip curling maliciously and he thrust his purple-blotched face close to his wife's, 'you loved a Royalist, did you not?'

For once her eyes met his resentful gaze calmly. 'That was a long time ago,' she said softly and not without a trace of sadness in her tone. 'A very long time ago.'

'But you have never forgotten him, have you?' her husband snarled. 'I remember—aaah, what matter? He's gone now, into exile. You'll never see him again.' He turned swiftly from her, marching from the room and slamming the heavy door behind him leaving his wife biting her trembling lip.

So Charmian's marriage was postponed and the weeks drifted into months. Not that she was allowed the opportunity of meeting any other suitor for her life was strictly ordered, secluded and sheltered.

Then in September 1658, the world that Joseph Radley had believed to be so secure began to crumble.

Oliver Cromwell died of pneumonia.

Joseph Radley was like a man possessed with an evil, fearful spirit. He stormed through the house like a wild boar, bellowing orders and then immediately countermanding them so that his servants were soon running in all directions in total confusion.

Elizabeth and Charmian looked at each other anxiously, but only Charmian was bold enough—now at 19, almost 20—to voice the question.

'What will happen now?'

'How should I know?' her father growled. 'His son, Richard, is to succeed. I will have to go to him. He is not the man his father was. He'll be the ruin of us all!'

Joseph Radley left Boston in a flurry and a fury, and peace settled upon the household after his departure.

Over the next few months news came from him spasmodically. Cromwell had nominated his son Richard as his successor, but some eight months later a hastily written letter arrived for Elizabeth Radley from her husband.

'... *He has been overthrown by the military chiefs led by his own brother-in-law, Fleetwood. We are in a state of chaos ...*'

Later, word came that after Parliament having been recalled and then six months later dissolved, the situation was growing worse daily. Once more England seemed on the brink of civil war.

Throughout the country from the nobility to the peasant farmer, men began to plan for the return of their King. Some brave souls threw off the mantle of Puritanism which they had been obliged to wear to ensure the safety of their families, put on their finery once more and grew their hair long, openly defying the strict Puritan laws.

Joseph Radley had been absent from home for over a year. Elizabeth and her daughter were taking a walk in the grounds surrounding their home—wrapped in warm cloaks against the sharp winter day—when they saw three horsemen riding through the gates and galloping towards the house.

' 'Tis your father,' Elizabeth said and immediately the look of fear which for the past months had been absent was back in her eyes.

'Come, Madam, pray do not be alarmed,' Charmian said determinedly and she put her arm through her mother's.

'We—we had better go and greet him, I suppose,' Elizabeth said and together they walked towards the house.

The stable-lads were already leading away the three steaming horses.

'They've been ridden mightily hard,' Charmian murmured, raising her eyebrows in surprise. Despite her father's harshness towards his family and servants, she had never before known him to misuse an animal.

Charmian and her mother entered the hall to see Joseph Radley pacing up and down, already shouting at his servants once more. The two men with him—strangers to Charmian—were standing near the huge fireplace holding out their hands towards the blazing logs.

'Ah, there you are, Wife,' Joseph said and Elizabeth went forward dutifully to greet her husband.

'We must leave for my sister's home. Our daughter's marriage must take place at once.'

Charmian felt as if an icy hand had closed around her heart and, for a moment, stilled its beating.

Joseph Radley flung his hands apart wildly. 'We must go there. We shall be safe there. Their home is like a fortress.'

'Safe? Joseph, why should we not be safe here, in our own home?'

Her husband stopped his restless pacing, but still breathing heavily, he said, 'The Royalists are in power again, at least, almost.' He glanced towards his two companions. 'Since Cromwell's death we have been on a downward spiral and now, General Monk, commanding the Scottish Army, has marched into London. The Rump Parliament tried to minimize his popularity by ordering that he should quell the rebels who have refused to pay taxes—' Again Joseph Radley resumed his pacing. 'But what did he do? He turned the tables on Parliament by forcing restoration of the full Parliament and in so doing brought about a Presbyterian majority! They mean to bring back Charles the Second, and Cromwell's men, those of us who are not turncoats—' his lip curled,—'are fleeing for our lives.' He gripped his wife's arm until she winced. 'But we are not done yet. There's still a chance. If we can but find a safe place and reorganize . . .'

A bark of wry laughter came from the taller of the two men standing near the fireplace. 'You're living in a fool's paradise, Radley. We are done—finished!'

'Never!' Joseph Radley bellowed, but the man merely stepped forward and bowed towards Elizabeth.

'Allow me to introduce myself, ma'am. My name is William Deane and this is my brother, Timothy.'

Elizabeth Radley acknowledged their presence, but quickly turned her attention back to her husband. 'Must we go? Surely to travel across open countryside would be far more dangerous than . . .'

William Deane turned away, leaving husband and wife to decide their future. His eyes fell upon Charmian waiting quietly in the background. 'Ah, you must be the charming Charmian.' He smiled, as if he had said something exceedingly witty. 'Your father has spoken of you, Miss Radley, but he omitted to mention your loveliness. I shall indeed take him to task upon the matter.'

He speaks with the smoothness of a snake, Charmian thought. Although she had met very few men in her young and sheltered life, she had an intuitive common sense which helped her to distinguish idle flattery from a sincere compliment.

William Deane was tall and thin with a dissolute look about him. His eyes were set too close together, his cheeks hollowed and his mouth small and mean.

'Allow me to introduce my brother, Timothy.' William Deane extended his arm and his brother almost leapt forward from his place by the fire.

'H-happy to make your acquaintance, M-miss Radley,' he stammered and Charmian was surprised to see him blush.

Timothy was very different. He was obviously much younger than William and was fair-skinned with a boyish face, blue eyes and a shy, hesitant manner. Charmian could see that he had little will of his own but merely followed the dictates of his brother.

' 'Tis settled then. We leave tomorrow,' Joseph Radley was saying.

William Deane turned. 'Tomorrow may be too late, Radley. They will be hot on our heels, I fear.' He laughed drily. 'I cannot imagine the Royalists allowing a general of Cromwell's Army, and one of the regicides to escape!'

Charmian watched her father closely. She had never seen him show fear and now, it seemed, his own life was in danger in the same way that during these last eleven years he had endangered many others—Royalist lives. She was interested—strangely dispassionately so—to see if he was afraid.

But his reaction was typical of the man. He became angry, the purple vein standing out vividly in his temple.

'Very well—we'll leave today.'

'But,' Elizabeth said haltingly, 'we must take a few things with us . . .'

'Just bring a few clothes—nothing else,' he rounded on her angrily. 'Do you want to see your husband butchered before your eyes? And your daughter—God knows what they would do to her!'

Elizabeth turned pale and gave a little cry of terror. 'Oh no, no, they wouldn't!'

'You think your Royalist friends will save you?' he sneered, never able to forget or forgive. 'I should not count upon it, my dear.'

They left within the hour. A coach and driver conveying Charmian and her mother and their maid, and the three men on horseback, leaving the rest of their servants to follow later.

During the journey across the flat Lincolnshire fenland from Boston to the comparative safety of Gartree Castle, they were in constant fear of being accosted by fervent Royalists, to say nothing of footpads who always roamed the lonely tracks. Recent heavy rains had left the highway a quagmire in places, so that their progress was slow and ponderous. At one point the coach stopped altogether and the ladies within felt the vehicle tip slowly to one side as one wheel sank into the mud.

You will have to get out—all of you, whilst we get it moving again.' Radley's face appeared at the door.

They clambered down into the muddy road.

'Ugh, the hem of my dress is all wet,' Charmian muttered in disgust, 'and the water has seeped through to my feet.'

'Then you should have worn something more sensible,' her father snapped.

'There was hardly time to think what to wear, let alone to put it on,' retorted Charmian angrily.

'How dare you answer me like that, Daughter, have a care or . . .'

'We are wasting time,' William Deane shouted through the rain. He was already trying to lever the coach out of the mud.

'Miss Radley,' Timothy Deane spoke shyly at her side. 'If—if you feel cold, I'd be happy to lend you m-my cloak.'

Charmian turned. 'Thank you, but I am sure you will need it on horseback more than I do seated in the coach. Besides . . .'

'Timothy, come and help, will you?' his brother shouted.

'Yes. I'm c-coming. I'm sorry, Miss Radley. I m-must go,' he apologized, backing away and almost tripping over his own feet.

Charmian felt the laughter bubbling up inside her. Timothy Deane was so shy and awkward and yet it would be cruel of her to ridicule him. It would be like whipping an affectionate puppy whose only desire was to please.

It took over an hour of struggling to free the coach, by which time tempers were frayed, the gentlemen and coachman splattered with mud, and the three women shivering with cold.

'Get in!' Radley bellowed. 'Let's be on our way.'

Three times the coach became stuck. Three times the ladies and their maid were obliged to wait in the cold whilst the men pushed and heaved to release it.

'There's a fog coming down now, as if we had not enough to contend with,' Radley muttered.

'Perhaps the fog will be to our advantage,' Charmian heard William Deane remark as she climbed back into the coach. 'It will give us cover.'

'Ay, you could be right,' her father replied.

'Thank you, Mr Deane,' Charmian smiled at Timothy who had given his hand to the ladies to help them re-enter the coach yet again.

Timothy Deane mounted his horse and as they moved off once more Charmian noticed that he rode close beside the coach nearest to the side where she was seated.

The swirling fog became thicker as they neared Gartree Castle. They passed through the village and began to climb the hill towards the Masons' home. There was an eerie silence about the place. The village had seemed deserted—too quiet almost—and now as they approached the mist-shrouded castle they could neither see nor hear any sign of life. No one came out from the guardhouse to impede their progress across the drawbridge and into the courtyard. The coach rattled on over the cobbled yard, echoing strangely as it drew closer to the castle rising out of the mist. Behind the vehicle clattered the horsemen, thankful that the unpleasant journey was over. They came to a halt in front of the doors leading into the castle and as they did so, Charmian heard the grinding of the machinery as the drawbridge was raised behind them. Peering out of the coach she saw, with a stab of fear, that two men had positioned themselves inside the bridge—two men with long, flowing hair, tall feathers in their hats and with their swords drawn.

They were King's men.

Chapter Four

At once Joseph Radley began to roar. 'What is the meaning of this? What . . .!'

Immediately, on every side of the courtyard stepped more soldiers, Royalists all, their swords drawn.

Charmian alighted from the coach and then assisted her mother. The gentlemen—her father and William and Timothy Deane—had dismounted and now each of them drew his sword. Timothy edged nearer to Charmian and stood protectively in front of her.

'There will be no need for bloodshed, Radley.' A deep voice boomed across the courtyard and Charmian turned to see two men standing at the doorway into the castle. She heard her mother's startled cry, saw her clasp her hand to her mouth and heard her frightened whisper. 'Geoffrey!'

Charmian looked again towards the two Royalists and memory stirred. Then, as her father shouted his defensive reply, Charmian knew who they were.

'I'll not surrender, Denholm. Never!'

'Sir Geoffrey Denholm,' Charmian murmured and her eyes went beyond him to the young man standing a pace behind him. 'And—and Campbell!'

The years had noticeably altered the Royalist father and son. Campbell had grown to full manhood. He was as tall and as broad as his father now, with a young man's lithe strength. His hair—his own she did not doubt—curled to his shoulders and he had grown a moustache and beard, the fashionable trait of the King's men. As she drew closer, Charmian caught a glimpse of a jagged scar down Campbell's right cheek, only partially hidden by his beard and long hair. But the greatest change seemed to be in his father. Sir Geoffrey had aged far more than the intervening years should have allowed. His hair, shorter than his son's, was thin and very grey. His once erect, broad frame seemed to stoop slightly and his right arm hung loosely, uselessly, it seemed, by his side, his hand covered by a glove. He held a sword, but in his left hand merely as a token. His voice, however, was still as strong and sure as Charmian remembered, as the memories of that first meeting came flooding back now that once more she stood before Sir Geoffrey and his son, Campbell Denholm.

'Put up your sword, Radley,' Sir Geoffrey was saying. 'We mean you and your family no harm . . .'

'Ha! My *family*—maybe not! But do you expect me to believe that the same good intention applies to me?'

Sir Geoffrey gave an exaggerated sigh, as if he were heartily tired of the whole business. 'Since you are determined to play the martyr, Radley . . .' He raised his voice and motioned to his own men. 'Take the men, but do not harm the ladies.'

From the comparative calm, the scene changed in a second to a courtyard of running men, of clashing swords and terrified shrieks from Elizabeth and her maid. Charmian, too stunned by the suddenness of it all to speak, merely stood watching. Then she felt strong arms about her and felt herself lifted bodily from the ground and carried into the castle.

She began to struggle. 'Put me down—leave me, I say. How dare you?'

Close beside her ear she heard his low chuckle and twisted her head round to find herself looking into the blue eyes of Campbell Denholm.

'If it is not my Princes Golden Hair grown up.'

He set her down upon her feet but he did not release her. Instead he held her by the shoulders at arm's length and leisurely surveyed her from head to toe. Charmian felt her cheeks grow hot under his bold scrutiny.

'Unhand me, sir. You forget . . .' she began angrily, but her hasty words were silenced by his mouth upon hers. She gasped as he drew her into his embrace, tilted back her head and kissed her. She felt herself respond, warmed by his strong arms, amazed at the sweet sensation which coursed through her whole being. It was the first time any man had kissed her full upon the mouth in this ardent manner and she was taken by surprise and disturbed by the tumult of her own untried emotions.

At last Campbell drew back but still held her in his arms, his face close to hers, his eyes boring deep into hers.

'How—how dare you?' But now her voice trembled and lacked conviction.

Campbell laughed at her anger. Offended, she struggled free from his embrace and stood facing him, her eyes flashing, her demure bonnet knocked awry and allowing her golden hair to cascade to her shoulders.

Campbell's eyes hardened. 'You are my prisoner, Charmian.'

'You have no right to call me by my given name. You ...'

'You forget,' he smiled mockingly. 'We are old friends.'

'Friends? How can we be friends? We are enemies!' she told him fiercely but the thought brought her no satisfaction. His eyes glittered dangerously.

'I see you have not grown up after all. You are a spoilt child in a woman's body,' he told her tauntingly. 'Well, I shall not be at your beck and call this time.'

'Oh!' Charmian cried furiously, but she could find no words to answer his insult.

At that moment the huge doors swung open and Charmian turned to see her father and the two Deane brothers brought into the great hall—prisoners of the King's men. Of her mother and Sir Geoffrey, there was no sign.

'Take them to the dungeons,' Campbell said curtly, and Charmian gasped.

'The dungeons? You mean to keep them down there?'

'I have told you,' Campbell faced her. 'They are our prisoners.'

'And what, pray, is to happen to me?' she asked boldly and with a rash sarcasm in her tone. 'Am I to be committed to the dungeons too?'

'Possibly, if you do not behave properly.'

Charmian stamped her foot but the action only produced a squelching sound and reminded her of her own discomfort.

'It seems,' Campbell remarked mockingly, eyeing the mud-stained hem of her skirt and cloak, 'that you would do well to change your clothing and bathe. Wentworth,' he called to one of his men, 'show Miss Radley to a bedchamber and see that a maid attends her.' Turning back to Charmian, he asked, 'Where is your mother?'

'How should I know,' Charmian snapped crossly. 'I expect Sir Geoffrey has carried her off somewhere.'

'Ha! I shouldn't be at all surprised!' Campbell murmured, and he laughed again, feeding the flame of her anger.

'Where is my aunt and uncle—and Joshua? Are they all in the dungeons already?'

'No. The whole castle is under guard and anyone who will give us their promise that they will not attempt to escape may move freely about the building and part of the grounds too, if they wish. But your father does not seem eager to comply.' Now Campbell's voice was laced with sarcasm.

'Perhaps,' Charmian told him haughtily. 'I shall not succumb either.' And with that she turned from him and swept away in what she hoped was a dignified manner.

In the seclusion of the bedchamber, Charmian began to take off her wet clothing but she was still smarting from what she considered to be Campbell's insolent behaviour. How different was the reality to her memory of him.

'I do not know why you are taking all this so calmly,' she said to her mother when Elizabeth Radley entered the room some time later. 'Don't you realize, we are prisoners of Royalists? Goodness knows what will become of us. Ugh!' She wrinkled her nose as she drew off her sodden pattens and hose. 'Nell, go and find some hot water at once. This mud is caked on my feet,' Charmian added.

'Hot water, miss. I doubt there will be *hot* water in this household, but I'll see what I can do.'

As the girl closed the door behind her, Elizabeth turned towards her daughter. 'No harm will come to any of us, my dear. We are fortunate that it is Sir Geoffrey Denholm here, and not some other Royalist.' A small, wistful smile played at the corners of her mouth.

Charmian opened her lips to make a sharp retort, but closed them again without uttering a word. She is glad he is here, Charmian thought with a sudden shock. Glad that they were all Sir Geoffrey's prisoners.

Later when they descended to the great hall once more, having bathed away the mud and changed into clean, dry garments, Charmian began to see that perhaps her mother had good reason to be thankful that their captor was Sir Geoffrey.

'We are not here by mere chance, my dear,' he told Elizabeth, whilst Charmian stood beside her mother's stool and listened quietly.

'I came here purposely because I thought that your husband would be most likely to seek the support of his sister and her somewhat fortress-like home. Elizabeth, the Puritans are being pursued as they once pursued us and I am afraid some Royalists whose own families were cruelly treated by Cromwell's men are now extracting their own revenge. That is not my way, but I am powerless to prevent it. All I could do was to ensure that you—and Charmian—did not fall into the hands of those now lusting for vengeance.'

There was only Charmian and her mother and Sir Geoffrey by the huge roaring log fire at one end of the great hall. Despite the vast coldness of the room, there was suddenly a curious intimacy between the three of them.

'We returned from France only three weeks ago from exile,' Sir Geoffrey continued. 'My wife stayed here in England all the time, but our estate was confiscated and given to a Puritan. Luckily Georgina was taken in by a yeoman farmer.' He smiled a little. 'A man who once worked for me and whom I helped some years back to obtain his own farm. He repaid his debt of gratitude in full by caring for Georgina in my absence. Not all old loyalties were forgotten—thank God—though the Parliamentarians have made life as difficult for them these past years as they possibly could.' He paused. 'And Georgina has been remarkably courageous in the way that she has managed all this time without either husband or son for help, not even knowing whether we still lived.'

Deliberately, it seemed, he glossed over the long years he and his son had spent in exile whilst not knowing how his wife fared under the rule of the Protector. But those years had left their scars on both father and son, even the innocent eyes of Charmian Radley could see and understand that much.

A shudder ran through Elizabeth and she looked down at her hands lying in her lap and murmured, 'Georgina has been a good wife to you.'

'Yes, yes, she has. I'll not deny that, but, if only . . .'

Charmian saw her mother look up quickly to meet his intense gaze. But then Sir Geoffrey sighed softly and whispered, 'Ah well, 'tis best left unsaid, eh?'

A small smile flickered across Elizabeth's face. It seemed as if she had the answer she sought, that she knew his meaning even if the words had not been spoken aloud.

But Charmian was mystified.

Sir Geoffrey was speaking again. 'They—Cromwell's men—tried poor Georgina sorely. They demanded fines and heavy taxes and such like acts of harassment. But now, we are back and very soon our young King will be here too and we shall have the monarchy restored.'

'What—what will happen to—to the Parliamentarians then?' Elizabeth Radley asked.

Sir Geoffrey sighed heavily. 'I put my faith in His Majesty. I trust that, like me, he wants no more bloodshed, but . . .'

'But . . .?' Elizabeth Radley prompted. His gentle eyes looked into her lovely face and he took her hand in his. 'My dear, the years of Puritan rule have wrought vast changes amongst many Royalists. Many have lost everything—their families, their homes and possessions. Some have been cruelly used, excessively so. The mood—the—the—' he hesitated, searching for the right word of explanation. 'The character of the Cavalier—the romantic, honourable figure, defending faith and virtue and freedom—has been obliterated by the years of harsh reality. And many—I regret to say—have become disillusioned and—dissolute. They seek revenge upon their oppressors. But I remain hopeful that when we once more have our King as our head, then things will improve. They are in the main good men at heart but have been sorely used.' He glanced down at his own useless right arm briefly, but even then he did not dwell upon his own afflictions. His gaze came back once more to Elizabeth Radley. It was as if his whole aim, his one thought, was to secure her safety.

'But surely,' Charmian spoke up for the first time. 'The King will demand an oath of allegiance from the Parliamentarians, will he not?'

Sir Geoffrey started and then turned to look at her. It was as if he had forgotten her presence for all the while they had been talking his gaze had been upon her mother's face.

'Yes, yes, my dear. I expect he will want that at the very least.'

'And if—if Cromwell's men will not give such a promise?'

Sir Geoffrey raised his shoulders fractionally. 'I'm afraid I cannot answer for the King, my dear.'

At that moment the strident voice of Mary Mason rang out from the far end of the hall 'Elizabeth, I have only just been informed of your arrival.'

Charmian saw Sir Geoffrey's expression harden as Mary Mason crossed the hall and came towards them.

'Well, Denholm, you may have inveigled the support of Elizabeth but you will never sway my brother or myself to your side. Of that I can assure you.' Scarcely pausing for breath, she rounded upon Charmian. 'And I trust, dear Niece—' The words of endearment were spoken mechanically with no tone of affection. 'That you are ready to fulfil your betrothal promise and unite our two families even more closely in the cause of our Faith.'

Charmian saw Sir Geoffrey's expression grow even more grim. 'Charmian,' he asked her. 'Do you wish to marry your cousin?'

Before she had even the time to think of a reply, Mary Mason cried, 'How dare you, sire? You may hold us prisoners, but you have no right to interfere in a family matter. No right at all.'

'I have no wish to see a girl as lovely as Charmian forced into a marriage she does not desire. Too much unhappiness has already been caused by such actions. What say you, Elizabeth?' His tone was noticeably more tender when addressing Elizabeth Radley.

'I . . .' Elizabeth began, but Mary Mason was not to be beaten.

'The betrothal was entered into many years ago. You witnessed it yourself, Sir Geoffrey—uninvited—did you not?'

'I did indeed,' Sir Geoffrey replied drily. 'When Charmian was but a child, scarcely aware of the implications of the promises she was being obliged to make. But now she is a woman and should be allowed to decide her future for herself.'

'Pah! Whoever heard of such a thing?'

Angrily Mary Mason turned away and walked back across the room with long, unfeminine strides. Sir Geoffrey watched her go. 'Poor Edward!' he murmured, referring to Mary's docile husband and his brother-in-law. 'How ever did he come to ally himself with such a scold?'

Joshua Mason had grown from being a fat boy to grossly overweight manhood. He was small and stockily built, his face round and florid—like his mother and his uncle, Joseph Radley. His face wore a perpetually sly expression and, meeting him again, Charmian shuddered with revulsion. Was this coarse glutton to be her husband?

'We are to be married then?' he remarked to Charmian as they dined later that evening. Charmian watched him hold a chicken bone with his fingers and tear the meat from it with his short, yellow teeth. Then deliberately he licked each finger so as not to miss the merest morsel. The action prompted a vague memory from their last meeting. Joshua's manners had not improved with the years between.

'Yes,' she replied now in a small voice.

From across the table she could feel Campbell Denholm's mocking eyes upon her, but she dare not look up. She dared not meet his gaze.

'Sooner the better, eh?' Joshua was saying.

'Oh, I don't know. Perhaps we should wait. I mean, my father . . .'

'Your father will be taken off to London as soon as the King returns,' Joshua said callously. 'We'd best get it done now. Denholm will let us hold the ceremony.'

'You—you think so?' Fear was flooding through her. She was caught helplessly in a trap and there was no one to help her.

Suddenly she rose from the table. 'Pray excuse me. I don't feel well.' She turned to leave the room.

Slyly, Joshua grinned. 'A maiden's modesty at the thought of becoming a bride, eh?' he leered, as Charmian hurried away feeling physically sick at the thought of becoming Joshua Mason's wife.

Chapter Five

Charmian had found the swing in the tree down by the river. Hunting around she found a long piece of broken branch and after a few moments' prodding and levering she had managed to make the swing fall down. Although the day was damp and cold, the mist still hanging over the countryside, Charmian had felt the need to escape from the confines of the castle walls. Now, happier than she had felt since her father's arrival home to their house in Boston, she seated herself on the swing and propelled herself backwards and forwards.

Unseen by Charmian, Campbell Denholm stood in the shelter of the trees watching her. He had seen her leave the castle and had followed, but now he hesitated to approach her. Her attitude towards him had been unfriendly—indeed it seemed she had tried to avoid him—for she seemed to spend most of the day in her bedchamber either alone or with her mother.

Higher and higher she swung, breathing deeply, feeling joyously free. Suddenly there was a crack as one of the ropes snapped and Charmian went hurtling through the air. Almost before she had hit the ground, Campbell was running towards her, 'Charmian!'

She was already stirring when he reached her and moaning. 'Oh dear, oh dear!' in a shaking voice.

With unexpected gentleness his strong hands felt her arms and shoulders, but his tone as he spoke to her was sharp. 'You foolish child! Didn't you realize the swing would be rotten? It won't have been used for years. Probably not since . . .' Fondly he was remembering the last time she had used that very swing.

'I'm all right,' Charmian muttered crossly. Her senses returning, she tried to scramble to her feet but she swayed unsteadily. Without another word Campbell swung her into his arms, ignoring her cry of protest and carried her up the slope towards the castle. He carried her into the main hall and immediately they were confronted by Mary Mason, who wore a gleeful expression which quickly turned to anger at the sight of Campbell with Charmian in his arms.

'What is the meaning of this?' she demanded.

'Charmian has had an accident,' Campbell told her shortly. 'The swing broke and she has suffered a nasty fall.' He set Charmian down on the floor, but still he kept his arms about her.

'Are you hurt?' The question from her aunt lacked genuine concern.

'Merely shaken, I think,' Charmian replied.

' 'Tis as well for I have found a magistrate who has agreed to marry you and Joshua the day after tomorrow.'

Pale already from her fall, Charmian gasped. The surroundings seemed to fall in upon her and everything went black. She would have crumbled to the floor had not Campbell's strong, supporting arm prevented it. Picking her up once more in his arms, her head resting against his broad shoulder, Campbell faced her aunt.

'Madam—if a Puritan magistrate sets foot in this castle, I shall arrest him!' And before she could make a reply, he was gone, leaving her open-mouthed whilst he carried Charmian to her bedchamber.

When Charmian opened her eyes again it was to see Campbell bending over her and her mother standing anxiously beside him. Charmian was lying on the truckle-bed where she slept. She struggled to sit up but her mother put her hand upon her shoulder and gently urged her to lie down again. 'Rest, my love,' she murmured.

Charmian glanced from her mother's worried face to meet Campbell's eyes. The tenderness faded from his brown eyes as he realized she was not hurt. Abruptly he turned away. 'Perhaps next time you will not be so thoughtless,' was his parting shot.

As he left the chamber, Charmian could not know of the agony

43

in Campbell Denholm's heart as he thought of her intended marriage to Joshua Mason. All through the terrible years of exile Campbell had kept the memory of the bright-haired girl locked within his heart. Yet now they were together again, he could not reach out to her, not like before. Perhaps the fault was his in part. The years had made him bitter, yet through it all he loved her still. He could not allow this marriage to take place. Somehow he would have to put a stop to it.

'My dear son, I sympathize with your feelings,' Sir Geoffrey was saying a short time later when Campbell had told him of Mary Mason's plans for Charmian's marriage and his own threat to her if she should try to carry them out. 'But I am not quite sure we have the power to arrest a priest.'

'It is not a priest coming, but a magistrate, if you please. She is not even to be given a marriage in church,' he said, glowering, but then added, 'but perhaps that is all to the good.'

'Poor child, poor child,' Sir Geoffrey murmured sadly. 'Just like her mother—sacrificed to satisfy her peers.'

'I shall not allow it!' Campbell stormed with the fierce confidence of youth. 'She is not going to marry that—that—aah!' Frustrated he clenched one fist and smacked it against the palm of his other hand. 'What *can* we do, sire?'

His father sighed and lifted his shoulders in a gesture of helplessness. 'There is nothing we can do by law until the King returns. However,' he added with a sudden grin. 'Mistress Mason is not to know that, now is she? Perhaps your threat will be sufficient to make her think again.'

It seemed, for the time being at least, that it was, for the magistrate did not appear the following day nor for several days and though Charmian passed the time in fear of his arrival, nothing happened.

Charmian suffered no injury from her fall except for a bruise or two, and on the second day she looked out of her bedroom window to see Timothy Deane being allowed to take exercise in the enclosed courtyard, though he was guarded by three Royalist soldiers. He looked a lonely figure, little more than a boy though he must be about her own age, she thought. He was slightly built with fair hair, grey eyes and a pale skin which looked even more sickly after his days and nights in the dank dungeon. Reaching for her cloak she went down to join him. The soldiers made no move to prevent her from falling into step beside their prisoner, though Charmian was conscious of their eyes upon them as she and Timothy walked around the courtyard.

'Charmian!' Timothy's face was alight with pleasure. 'How good it is to see you.' He held out his hands to her and briefly clasped them. Then embarrassed, he let them go. 'Are they treating you w-well?'

'Yes, yes, they are. But you—and the others, my father and your brother—are they treating you well?'

He gave a wan smile. 'Tolerably so. We have plenty to eat though the surroundings are not exactly comfortable.'

'If only my father had not been so—so obstinate, maybe none of you would have been imprisoned.'

'Maybe not.' But there was doubt in his tone.

'Is my father still as—as determined in his beliefs?' she asked, hesitating over her choice of words, wanting to say fanatical and yet fearing the word would sound disloyal to her own father.

There was a pause while Timothy appeared to consider. 'It is strange you should ask that b-because—I can't be sure, but I wonder if they—your father and my brother, I mean—are beginning to—I don't know, not give up their cause exactly, but they have talked and discussed the situation all the time and often they talk in whispers and deliberately exclude me.'

'Why should they do that?'

'I don't know. Oh I expect they think I am just too young—or too weak. I have always just b-blindly followed my b-brother.'

They walked on in silence.

'Do you think they could be considering swearing allegiance to the King?' Charmian asked at last. 'Surely with King Charles's return the Parliamentarian cause must be lost?'

'I really do not know.' Timothy glanced at her, a question in his eyes. 'You—you sound as if you believe that to be so. Have these—these Cavaliers—' He still used the derisory name with a vehemence which surprised Charmian coming from the lips of the shy young man. '—persuaded you against us already?'

Charmian felt a sudden twinge of guilt. Under Sir Geoffrey's gentle protection, watching his obvious caring attitude towards her own mother, and—despite her protestations otherwise—drawn by Campbell's flamboyant handsomeness, Charmian realized she had begun to compare the rigidity of her father's Puritanical ways with the easier—Joseph Radley would say sinful—life-style of the Royalists. They were her enemies, Charmian reminded herself. It was wicked of her to have allowed herself to be duped by their kindness.

Her chin came up stoutly, 'Of course not,' she declared, 'But what can I—we—do? We are their prisoners just as much as you, even though we are not confined to the dungeons.'

At that moment a voice rang across the courtyard. 'Here, Puritan, get below again. Too much sun will damage your sinless soul,' the soldier laughed vulgarly. 'And walking with this lovely maid'll give you lustful ideas.' He laughed again.

'Charmian,' Timothy cried eagerly as the soldier pushed him towards the steps leading down into the dungeon. 'Please—will you meet me here again tomorrow?'

'Yes, of course,' she smiled at him. As she turned towards the door into the castle, they waved once more to each other before he disappeared from the sunlit courtyard into the dank coldness underground.

From a small window above Mary Mason watched them with growing resentment. She was even more determined that the marriage between her son and her niece should take place as soon as possible.

'If it were not for these damned Cavaliers,' she muttered angrily to herself, 'they'd be married by now.'

And Mary Mason was not the only one who had watched the meeting between Charmian and Timothy Deane. At a window on the opposite side of the courtyard stood the silent, motionless, figure of Campbell Denholm watching them walking together.

He was powerless to still the jealousy which tore at his heart.

The next afternoon Charmian watched for Timothy to appear in the courtyard and as soon as she saw him she hurried down to join him, but this time a soldier barred her way. 'Sorry, miss. We've had orders that the prisoner is not to be allowed to talk with you.'

'On whose orders?' Charmian demanded hotly.

The young soldier hesitated then said, 'The young master's, miss.'

Campbell! This was too much! What harm could there be in her walking and talking with Timothy Deane in full view of anyone who cared to watch? She was making no clandestine meeting. Campbell must have been watching yesterday from the castle windows.

She glanced across at Timothy and nodded towards the soldier. 'It seems I am not allowed to speak with you.'

Disappointment was on the boy's face. As she turned to go, he called after her, 'Charmian—your father sent a message. He wants to see you.'

'I doubt I shall be allowed to now, but I will try. Please to tell him that.'

Thoughtfully she returned inside. It would be useless to ask Campbell, she thought, but perhaps his father.

'Where is Sir Geoffrey?' she demanded of her mother as she burst into the small room where Elizabeth sat sewing. Startled by her daughter's sudden entrance, Elizabeth dropped her embroidery, but it was Mary Mason, from her seat in the window, answered, 'And why should you wish to speak with him?'

Charmian rounded on her. 'If you must know, I wish to visit my father, and as it seems Campbell Denholm is set upon my having no discourse with his prisoners, I thought perhaps his father might be more lenient.'

Mary Mason smiled maliciously. 'I doubt it, but you can try.'

'I intend to do so. Well, do you know where he is?'

'In the great hall, I believe,' Mary Mason replied and Charmian went at once to find him.

'Please may I have a word with you, Sir Geoffrey?' Charmian

stood before him, deliberately ignoring Campbell who was I seated on the opposite side of the blazing fire.

'Of course, my dear.' Sir Geoffrey rose and placed a stool for her. And when she hesitated, for it was not customary for a young Puritan to be seated in the presence of their elders, he said kindly, 'Pray, sit down. Now what may I do for you?'

'I would speak with you alone, sir, if you please.' Still she had not moved to sit down and she refused to look towards Campbell. She was so afraid that the sight of him would stir memories of all the happy moments they had shared together—so long ago it seemed now—and that her resolve would weaken. She was determined to hold herself aloof from him. He was her enemy, was he not? she told herself fiercely.

She felt Campbell move behind her and knew that he had risen and left them alone.

'Now will you sit down,' Sir Geoffrey said gently, and Charmian felt her resolution crumbling. It was impossible to continue feeling resentment and anger against someone so courteous and charming.

'Please—will you allow me to visit my father?'

Sir Geoffrey's eyes were upon her face and then he asked softly, 'Is it really your father you wish to visit—or young Deane?'

Charmian gasped and felt embarrassment creep into her face. 'No—no, I mean, yes. It is my father. He—he sent word by Timothy Deane that he would like to see me.'

Sir Geoffrey's eyebrows rose quizzically. 'Did he indeed? Well, I see no harm in your being allowed to visit him.'

'Thank you.'

'Come, I will take you there myself.'

They descended the stone steps into the dungeons and walked along a dismally lit passage. At the far end, outside a heavy door, stood two Royalist soldiers.

'Miss Radley is to be allowed to visit her father,' Sir Geoffrey told them, and then he turned to Charmian. 'I trust you understand the necessity for being locked in with them whilst you visit? My men will let you out as soon as you are ready to leave.'

He turned to his soldier. 'I charge you to bring Miss Radley safely back to me.'

'Sir!' The soldier responded smartly. Charmian noticed with relief that it was not the man from the courtyard the previous day who was being charged with her safe conduct.

The soldier unlocked the door and pushed it open and then stood aside for Charmian to enter.

'Radley,' Sir Geoffrey called. 'You have a visitor.'

She stepped into the cold, bare cell and blinked, trying to accustom her eyes to the dimness.

'Charmian—my dear.'

She stopped in astonishment. It was the first time she could ever remember having heard her father use her given name. Always he had called her Daughter—and her mother Wife—in that cold, authoritarian manner with which he had ordered all their lives. He was coming towards her, his hands outstretched to greet her, a smile upon his face. He took her hands in his and led her towards a bench seat set against the stone wall.

'Come and sit down, my dear, I have much to say to you. I'm sorry,' he added apologetically, 'that I cannot offer you more comfortable surroundings.' For a moment conflicting emotions fought for expression on his face, but with a supreme effort he continued to smile. 'Our captors thought this accommodation the most suitable for us.'

William Deane came and stood close beside her. 'Are they treating you kindly?' he asked, smiling too, though it was more a baring of his teeth for the smile did not reach his eyes.

'Yes—yes, we are quite comfortable, thank you,' Charmian murmured, still mystified by the enormous change in her father's manner towards her.

At her words Joseph Radley gave a snort of wry laughter, 'I thought as much ...' he began and then stopped abruptly as Charmian saw William Deane touch his shoulder warningly. Radley cleared his throat and sat down on the bench which creaked under his weight.

Charmian glanced around the dark, dank place, her eyes searching for Timothy Deane. He was sitting crouched in a corner, his eyes wide, his face pale—almost white. Charmian cried out and half rose from the bench as if to run to him. 'Oh Timothy—are you ill?'

But her father's fingers grasped her arm and pulled her back down on to the bench.

'Mr Deane,' she said to William. Your brother—he—he looks ill!' Here in this cold prison he looked far worse than he had done in the open air on the previous day.

William Deane glanced briefly in the direction of his brother. 'Fear, Miss Radley, is an unhealthy bedfellow. My brother believes we may all shortly meet our deaths!'

Charmian gasped and turned a little paler herself. 'Oh surely not. Sir Geoffrey cannot mean to harm us.'

Her father looked at her soberly. 'There are many things you do not yet understand, my dear child. No—no,' he shook his head, 'you are no longer a child—you are a young woman and I must treat you as such.' He gave an exaggerated sigh. 'Sir Geoffrey Denholm is my enemy. He has been this many a long year. I know he seeks my death.'

Charmian was silent, her gaze upon her father's face. She was remembering, not so very long ago, his glee when Sir Geoffrey and his King had been exiled, and, more shadowy, the memories came back of the ambush of the Royalist coach, and Sir Geoffrey and Campbell as her father's prisoners. Now the situation was reversed, he nevertheless seemed to expect leniency from the very men he had previously hounded from their country because of their differing beliefs. She became aware that her father was speaking again and her shock at his revelations was far greater than the surprise she was feeling at his changed attitude towards her.

'Many years ago, Sir Geoffrey tried to seduce your mother. Oh I am sure she did not succumb to him.' He patted his daughter's hand. 'I would not want you to think badly of your mother.'

'I would never do that,' Charmian said with such a quiet conviction that her father glanced at her sharply. For an instant his face darkened and the vein in his temple began to throb.

'Radley . . .' William Deane's voice came softly—warningly—out of the shadows.

'Yes—yes,' her father snapped at him and then taking a deep breath turned once more to his daughter. 'Quite so, my dear, quite so. As I say, your mother had been promised to me by her guardian, as a young girl, but Denholm turned her head till she fancied herself in love with him. She was an innocent, impressionable girl who was flattered by his charm, his—his curling hair and Cavalier manners . . .' Hatred and bitterness crept into his tone.

Once more William Deane moved a little closer and Joseph Radley stopped, cleared his throat and began again.

Recollections were flitting through Charmian's mind. Hazy memories from her first visit to Gartree Castle as a child—her mother and Sir Geoffrey in the arbour near the river, talking together earnestly. And now, even though he was their captor, her father's enemy, there was no mistaking Sir Geoffrey's gentleness towards Elizabeth Radley, his tender concern for her comfort and safety, and even, there was no denying it, the happiness that shone from her mother's face when Sir Geoffrey was near. Charmian swallowed painfully. She wanted so much to believe that her dear mother would do no wrong, but she had seen with her own eyes things which confirmed her father's words.

'So you see, my dear,' he was saying. 'Denholm—and his son—are my sworn enemies. Deane and I have been talking. It seems as if the King will regain his throne now that Cromwell is gone. We—we think it best—to—to swear our allegiance to His Majesty.'

Charmian gasped and Timothy Deane scrambled to his feet. 'What?' His voice was a hoarse whisper. 'But you said you would never—ever—swear . . .'

William Deane strode across the floor. 'Silence, boy, if you know what's good for you,' he said roughly.

'But, Brother, you said you would rather face the axe than ever swear allegiance to the King!'

William raised his arm and Timothy cowered beneath an expected blow. 'Hold your tongue!' the elder brother growled.

Charmian felt confused. She could understand Timothy's feelings for she herself was astounded at her father's statement.

'You mean—you mean you are going to give up your beliefs? You are going to—to . . .'

'No—no,' her father said. 'We believe—William and I—that if we could talk to the King we could make him understand. We could ask him for the right for people to follow their own particular religious beliefs without persecution, provided that those beliefs in no way injured His Majesty and the Crown. Do you understand me, Charmian?'

Again he used her name. So unused was she to hearing it upon her father's lips, that each time Charmian started in surprise.

'I think so,' she said hesitantly. This was such a swift, unexpected and complete change of heart on her father's part, such a change of manner towards her, that she could scarcely believe any of it to be real. He was leaning towards her, talking earnestly, his fingers grasping her wrist. 'But Denholm will seek our deaths, I know it. If only we could get to the King! Charmian, will you help us? Will you?'

'I don't know how I can,' she faltered. William Deane came then and knelt down before her. Behind him, Timothy inched closer, his eyes wide and fearful, as amazed as Charmian at what he was hearing.

'Miss Radley, you can help us to escape, if only you will. You and your aunt.'

'We thought it best to ask to see you. They will not suspect you, but,' Joseph Radley laughed, 'Denholm would at once suspect we were plotting if my sister were to ask to visit us.'

'But—but I don't understand what I can do.'

'Tell only your aunt of what we plan. She will provide some potion to put in a drink for the guards. Nothing to harm them,' Joseph Radley explained, 'just to make them sleepy.'

'But . . .'

'What you must do is this,' William added, 'Come to see us every day before nightfall, each time bringing some wine for the guards.'

'The cellar at the opposite end of this passage,' her father put in, 'near to the steps, 'tis stocked with wine. Bring some each day, then when they have become accustomed to your visits . . .'

'Indeed, they will begin to look forward to your coming, slip the draught into the drink,' William said.

'Then—then what must I do?' Charmian asked nervously.

'You will make a short visit that evening and then return later, when the draught has had time to take effect and when the rest of the household is abed, to let us out.'

'I understand,' Charmian said slowly, 'and—and you intend to go to the King and swear allegiance to him?' Still she could not believe that this was so and could not help but ask to hear it yet again from their own lips.

'We mean to seek out His Majesty,' William Deane said solemnly. 'Indeed we do. Will you help us?'

Behind him, out of the darkness, she saw the terrified eyes of Timothy Deane waiting for her response. He did not deserve to die and she was sure that Campbell—if not his father—was bent on revenge. And if what her father had said was true and she did not help them, they were sure to die.

Slowly Charmian nodded.

Surprised though she was by the remarkable change in her father, still she believed him, though Mary Mason's reaction on hearing of the plan rekindled some of the doubts in Charmian's heart.

'I am delighted to hear you are helping your father. I had grave fears about your loyalty to our cause, my dear niece, but now . . .'

'Oh no, Aunt Mason, you misunderstand. My father and the Deanes wish to swear their allegiance to His Majesty. But—but they fear—I mean—my father believes that Sir Geoffrey is his enemy and that he seeks my father's death. But if they can reach His Majesty, then they are sure he will show mercy.'

For a moment violent rage flashed in Mary Mason's eyes. 'I would never have believed . . .' she began and then after a moment's thought she said, 'And that was what your father told you, did he? Come now, Niece, tell me his exact words.'

'If I help them to escape, he said, they plan to seek out the King.'

'Aaah,' Mary Mason seemed to relax and she began to smile. 'In that case, then, my dear, we must help them, must we not?'

'Yes,' agreed Charmian, but somewhere in her heart there was still a nagging doubt.

Over the next week or so Charmian visited her father and his two fellow prisoners each evening just before darkness fell. Each time she took with her a flagon of wine, and as William Deane had predicted the soldiers soon greeted her arrival with enthusiasm.

During that week, Lady Denholm arrived at Gartree Castle and though Charmian observed Lady Denholm and her mother closely, to her surprise the two women were remarkably friendly towards each other and yet even in his wife's presence, Sir Geoffrey's gaze would linger upon Elizabeth Radley's face. Perhaps Lady Denholm does not know, does not suspect, that there was once anything between her husband and my mother, Charmian mused, watching them.

'Charmian.' She jumped as Campbell spoke softly behind her. 'I have not seen you—not to speak with—' he added pointedly, 'since your fall. I trust you are quite recovered?'

At once her face became a stiff mask of indifference. 'Quite. I thank you, sir.'

She made as if to move away from him but suddenly he grasped her wrist and twisted her around to face him. She cried out at the pain in her arm. 'Let go of me!'

His face was close to hers. 'Why are you avoiding me? You seem to find plenty of time to visit that—that whey-faced Puritan in the dungeon.'

Charmian gasped, her eyes wide. 'I don't know what you mean.'

'I think you know very well what I mean.'

She swallowed and tried to still the wild beating of her heart. She could think of no sharp retort to make and she was so afraid he would begin to suspect the real reason behind her visits to the dungeon if she were to deny his accusations.

Better to let him think her interest lay in Timothy Deane than that she should risk exposing her father's daring plan.

Twisting her wrist free of his grasp, she turned, picked up her skirts and fled from the brooding eyes of the handsome Campbell Denholm.

Chapter Six

'Tomorrow night. It must be tomorrow night!' Her father took hold of her arm when she visited the cellar that evening. Charmian winced as he held the very wrist which was still sore from Campbell's rough treatment. She swallowed the fear which rose in her throat at the thought of what she must do, and nodded.

'We dare not wait any longer. If Denholm were to decide suddenly to remove us to London, all would be lost.'

'But—but if the King has not yet returned—what—what will you do?' Charmian asked. She saw a glance pass between her father and William Deane.

'We shall hide out somewhere until we hear that he has returned,' William Deane said swiftly.

As she left the cellar, Timothy shyly put his hand upon her arm. 'Charmian—t-take care,' he whispered anxiously.

'I will,' she promised and smiled at him, but on the boy's pale face there was no smile in response.

'Will this make them sleep for long enough, do you think?' Charmian asked as her aunt pressed the flagon of wine into her hands. Mary Mason's eyes sparkled. 'Oh yes—they'll sleep quite long enough, my dear.'

'But it will not hurt them—cause them any pain?' Charmian persisted.

'Oh no. They will know nothing about it, I assure you.'

This was the part that Charmian did not like. What if her aunt had put in the wrong amount of sleeping-draught? Too little and the guards would not sleep. Too much and . . . But her mind shied away from that thought.

'Aha, here's the pretty Puritan maiden,' one of the guards greeted her as she approached them that night, and he seized the flagon from her. 'Here's to you, my pretty maid,' he laughed and raised it in the air. Charmian smiled weakly, trying to still the trembling in her limbs. She felt sure they must see her shaking hands, but they were too intent upon the ruby wine.

Inside the cell, her father hurried towards her. 'Is it done?' he whispered eagerly.

Charmian nodded.

'Good, good. Now you must not stay long—just in case the draught works quickly. If they make any comment upon your leaving so soon, say—say you have a malaise, then go straight to your room and wait a good hour, or more if needs be. Then return here and take the keys from the guards and open the door. We will do the rest.'

'My aunt said to tell you she will arrange for three horses to be saddled and waiting outside the main courtyard gate.'

'Good, good.'

'But how do you plan to get past the guards on the main gate?' Charmian asked. 'There are two posted there every night.'

In the dim light, she saw William Deane smile. 'We have that all planned, Miss Radley, never fear. Now, I think you should go.'

'Going already, miss,' one of the guards remarked in surprise.

'Yes—I—I have—I am very tired.'

'Here—take some of this wine,' said the other, holding out the flagon towards her.

' 'Twill help you sleep.'

Charmian gave a startled gasp and gazed fearfully at the wine for a moment and then pushed it away. 'No—no, thank you.' And she hurried up the dark passage, their laughter ringing in her ears.

Over two hours later Charmian was once again creeping down the steps to the dungeons. She was later than she had been told because Sir Geoffrey had not retired to his room until late. She slipped into the first room—the one where all the wine was stored—and listened for any sound from the guards. She could hear a low murmur of voices, punctuated by an occasional laugh—obviously they had not fallen asleep yet.

What should she do? Return to her room and wait a little longer or stay here and listen for when all became quiet? She did not relish the thought of sneaking back through the darkened castle, risking discovery. Perhaps it would be safer to stay here. Quietly she moved into a corner of the cell behind the racks of wine in case the guards should walk up and down the passage and glance in. The minutes ticked by and another hour passed whilst she huddled, cold and more than a little frightened in the damp cellar—waiting.

Then she heard some strange sounds—the noise of someone groaning and then a thud.

' 'Ere, what's the matter?' a voice said, but the only reply was a cry of agony.

'Oh my God,' came the voice again. 'Oh what is it . . .?'

Then he too gave a sharp cry of pain.

Charmian closed her eyes and almost groaned aloud too. Her aunt had promised that the sleeping-draught would cause no pain and now, from the sounds she could hear, the two guards were writhing in agony on the floor.

'Get—help!' she heard one say feebly and then he moaned again. But there was no reply from his companion.

Charmian found that she had crouched down in a corner, her hands clenched and tears were running down her face. Her aunt had promised her the Royalist soldiers would feel no pain!

All was quiet now and then she heard an urgent whisper come from the locked dungeon at the end of the passage. 'Charmian! Charmian, are you there?'

Stiffly, she rose and reluctantly went down the passage. The two guards were lying on the rough stone floor, their mouths hanging open, their eyes wide and staring with an expression of sheer agony. Charmian pressed trembling fingers to her lips to stop herself from crying out. She stood staring down at the twisting forms.

'Charmian—the keys! Hurry!' her father urged.

She did not want to touch them, but the keys were fastened to the belt of one of the guards.

'Quickly girl,' her father's voice was becoming impatient. 'Get the keys!'

Charmian's fingers straggled with the buckle on the man's belt, cringing every time she touched his body. The belt opened and the keys rattled on to the floor. She picked them up and then stood a moment looking down at the man.

'He—he's not breathing,' she cried out in alarm.

'Hush. Do you want to waken the whole castle?' Joseph Radley whispered fiercely, stretching out his hand through the bars in the door. 'Open this door!'

Wildly she turned to look at her father. 'But—he's not breathing. Is he—he's not dead?' Her voice rose again with hysteria.

'The door, girl. Open the door, damn you!'

Now her whole body was shaking so much, the blood pounding in her ears, that she could scarcely insert the huge key in the lock. But at last she did so and the door swung open. At once Joseph and William Deane were out of the cellar and stepping over the bodies of the guards without even glancing down at them whilst Charmian fell back against the wall, unable to drag her horrified gaze away from the two men lying so still now upon the floor.

Timothy had come to stand by her side.

'Oh Timothy—I did not know. She—she promised it would not harm them.'

'Don't cry, Charmian, p-please ...' Before he could say more, Charmian felt her father grasp hold of her and push her in front of him along the passage, William Deane had unstrapped the swords of the two guards, tossing one to Joseph and keeping the other for himself. 'We must get one for Timothy from somewhere,' he murmured.

They moved up the passage. William Deane in the lead with Joseph Radley, Charmian and Timothy following. Stealthily they climbed the stone steps and came up into the courtyard. The night was crisp and sharp with a brilliant full moon, so that everything could be clearly seen.

'Curse it,' muttered William Deane, 'we could have done without so much light.'

Keeping to the shadows they crept round the edge of the courtyard.

'Let me go back now,' whispered Charmian. 'I have done what you asked of me. I can be of no more use to you.'

'That is where you are wrong, Daughter. You are our means of escape. You are coming with us!'

'No, no,' Charmian cried out, but at once her father clamped his hand roughly over her mouth. 'Be quiet.'

'How many guards are there on the bridge?' William Deane whispered.

'I can only see two.'

'Then it looks like a straight fight. Leave the girl with Timothy.'

'Here—hold her. And don't let her go or it'll be the worse for all of us,' Joseph Radley said.

Charmian felt herself thrust roughly into Timothy's arms.

'P-please, don't call out,' he whispered in her ear. 'I don't want to hurt you. Charmian—I'm sorry—I didn't know this was going to happen, please believe me.'

Sobbing with fear, Charmian did not know what to believe. She watched as William Deane and her father moved stealthily towards the guards, who were taken by surprise when the two prisoners leapt from the shadows. Joseph Radley thrust his sword into the chest of one and though the second put up a fight for a few moments; he was quickly overpowered by William Deane. Charmian screamed and Timothy was forced to cover her mouth again.

'The drawbridge,' Joseph hissed and picking up both weapons of the dead Royalist guards, he beckoned to Timothy. 'Bring her here. Here's a sword for you.'

The noise of the brief scuffle and Charmian's scream had been enough to disturb someone in the castle. As the drawbridge rattled down and the escaping prisoners, with their hostage, ran out, Sir Geoffrey and his son appeared in the doorway and began to run across the courtyard. Other figures—Elizabeth Radley and Mary Mason—appeared only moments later.

'The horses! Where are the horses?' Joseph demanded wildly.

'There. By the wall,' William shouted. Then, as he saw that they were being pursued, Joseph Radley once more took hold of his daughter from Timothy and turned to face Sir Geoffrey and Campbell. The bright moon lit the scene with cruel brilliance as the opponents faced each other.

'Come no nearer, Denholm,' he warned, holding his sword towards them. 'Or I'll cut her throat!'

'Damn you, Radley!' Sir Geoffrey muttered and behind him Charmian now saw the figures of her mother and Mary Mason, cloaks thrown hastily over their nightgowns.

'Joseph, Joseph, don't harm her!' Elizabeth cried frantically. 'Please!'

'Bring the horses,' Joseph shouted.

'What are you about, Radley?' Sir Geoffrey demanded, whilst Joseph mounted the horse and William Deane held Charmian.

'What am I about?' Joseph replied mockingly. 'I intend to go to meet your King, Denholm. I intend to swear allegiance to His Majesty!' Now there was open sarcasm in every word.

Sir Geoffrey's wry laughter rang out in the clear night air. 'Ha! Do you expect me to believe that?'

'My daughter believes it, don't you, Charmian? That is why she helped us to escape.'

Campbell gave a bellow of rage and made as if to leap forward, but his father held him back. Joseph Radley leant down from his horse.

'Lift her up here in front of me,' he commanded William Deane and Charmian felt herself being hoisted up to sit in front of her father. William and Timothy mounted the other two horses.

Sir Geoffrey's eyes burned with rage. 'You'll pay for this, Radley, by God, you will pay for this. How can you use your own daughter? You're inhuman!'

Joseph laughed, the noise shrill in Charmian's ear so close to his mouth. 'My daughter! Ay—she's my daughter, though I don't doubt her mother wished her yours!'

Sir Geoffrey stepped forward a pace, but Joseph turned his sword and held it close to Charmian's throat. 'Come no nearer, Denholm, or I'll kill her.'

Charmian heard a high-pitched scream and saw her mother run forward. 'No, Joseph, no. Don't harm her. I have done no wrong. I swear it. Please!' Her hands groped for the bridle as the horses became restless with all the noise and shouting. 'Please, Joseph—please leave Charmian here.'

'No, she comes with us. That's the only way we can be sure we shall not be followed. Get out of my way, Wife.' And as he spoke Charmian felt him move his legs and kick the horse, but the animal, with Elizabeth Radley's hands still clinging to its bridle, rose in the air on its hind legs, its forelegs flailing above her.

Sir Geoffrey was already moving forward lunging himself towards her mother. Charmian watched in horror as Elizabeth fell to the ground and Sir Geoffrey threw himself across her at the moment the horse's hooves came crashing down. Charmian screamed and began to struggle wildly, but her father's arm was like an iron band about her. Now holding the reins in the same hand in which he held his sword, Joseph controlled his horse and urged it forward.

'Madam, oh Mother,' Charmian cried in anguish, stretching out her hands towards her. As Joseph spurred the horse, Charmian's last image was of Campbell bending over the still figures on the ground.

There was no escape for Charmian. Her father held her strongly. Down the hill the horses galloped and through the village. It was a painful ride for Charmian—seated in front of her father, his arm like an iron band round her. Unable to ride comfortably or properly, she was soon bruised and shaken. But her physical discomfort was nothing compared to her shattered emotions. The horrific scene she had just witnessed had left her numb. She did not know what to think or believe or whom to trust. She had believed her father and though he was still insisting that it was his intention to swear allegiance to the King, Sir Geoffrey Denholm had not believed him. But these thoughts were pushed to the back of her mind. The only thing she could think of was her mother. The dreadful picture was constantly before her eyes of her mother lying on the ground, the horse's hooves trampling down upon her and the man who had tried to shield her, the man who loved her so much that without a second's hesitation he had risked his own life to try to protect her.

Then they had lain still upon the ground with Campbell bending over them.

Campbell!

A shudder ran through her whole being as she thought of Campbell. How he would despise her now. She could never bear to face him again. She would rather die—now—than have to face the anger, the condemnation, in his eyes.

Where was that gentleness she had once seen in his eyes for his Princess Golden Hair? Was it really gone for ever? Had the years of exile embittered him so much that there was none of that tenderness he had once shown towards a little girl left in his nature? Tears coursed down her face, whilst the galloping horse knocked the breath from her body.

They had passed through the village unhindered and were out into the open countryside. Charmian became aware that William Deane had ridden closer to them and was shouting something to her father and pointing at her. Her father nodded and shouted back, 'Two miles more.'

They rode on.

An inn came into view, and Charmian felt their pace begin to slow.

'Ride on and get another horse saddled for her,' Joseph bellowed to William who nodded and spurred his own horse ahead.

Some minutes later, Joseph and Charmian and Timothy halted outside the small wayside inn where a boy was already leading a horse from the stable whilst William Deane could be seen pressing coins into the palm of the stout landlord standing in his nightshirt in the doorway.

'Come on, come on,' her father roared glancing behind him every few seconds—no doubt fearing that they would be followed. But, Charmian thought, Campbell would not follow. He will not care what happens to me now. He will want no more to do with me now or ever. He will never forgive me for what I have done this night.

The thought brought fresh tears to her eyes.

Chapter Seven

Charmian was wrong.

They had ridden scarcely another half-mile after the brief stop at the inn. Charmian was now riding on a horse of her own though through its bridle was linked a long leather strap which her father held along with his own reins. Although Charmian's horse could move easily, it was attached to her father's mount in this way so that she could not escape.

Suddenly, she heard a shout and heard her father say, 'The Devil take him! He's followed us.'

Charmian looked back over her shoulder and saw a lone horseman galloping a short distance behind them. It was Campbell, she knew. Slowly he was gaining on them.

Joseph Radley must have come to a sudden decision, for he slowed the horses and stopped, then the four riders turned to face the one man who now came to a halt some twenty paces away.

Radley, William Deane and Timothy had all drawn their swords and Campbell Denholm now did likewise. Grimly the men faced each other in the half-light of early morning, whilst Charmian waited, her heart beating painfully, fearfully.

'Radley—let Charmian go,' Campbell bellowed. 'And I'll pursue you no further, whatever your evil intentions towards my King may be.'

'Never!' roared her father. 'And if you come one step nearer I'll kill her!'

The point of his sword was suddenly near Charmian's throat. A small cry escaped her lips—one more of surprise than fear—that her own father should really mean to threaten her life. She dared now, for the first time, to take a look at Campbell's face and as she did so she drew breath sharply.

Never in her whole life had she seen anyone so angry; not even her ill-tempered father had ever looked so menacing, so frightening. Campbell dismounted and walked slowly, deliberately towards them, his eyes blazing, his handsome mouth tight, his firm jaw unyielding.

With intense deliberation he said, 'You harm one hair of her head, Radley, and you're a dead man!'

Joseph laughed. 'Oh, Sir Cavalier and no mistake!'

Suddenly, Timothy Deane turned his horse about and came up behind Radley and Charmian. Pushing his horse between their mounts, he raised his sword and with one swift downward stroke, he severed the leather thong tying Charmian's horse to her father's. 'Ride, Charmian. Go!' Timothy shouted, and at the sudden noise, her horse leapt forward towards Campbell before Radley had realized what was happening, but William Deane leapt forward and caught the reins of Charmian's horse before Campbell could reach her. Deane dragged the girl from her mount and on to his own and held her pinioned close to him, his left arm tight across her breast, his sword close to her throat.

At the same moment, with a bellow of rage, Radley brought his sword round and knocked Timothy Deane to the ground. 'Traitor!' he roared. 'You young pup, I'll. . .' Charmian screamed as her father threw himself from his horse and made as if to plunge his sword through Timothy's heart, but William Deane shouted warningly, 'Radley—he's my brother. Harm him and you'll not live long enough for time to regret it.'

The point of Radley's sword wavered uncertainly for an instant above the boy's chest, and then with a low growl of frustration he swung away, and sheathed his sword with a swift and angry movement.

There came the sound of galloping hoofbeats and Sir Geoffrey and two officers drew level with Campbell, reined in and dismounted. But their arrival, their swords, their bravery, were as futile as Campbell's own as helplessly they watched the lethal blade only an inch from Charmian's throat.

She cried out weakly, just once, 'Campbell!' and in that utterance of his name was all her desperate longing, her fear, her pleading for his forgiveness. Involuntarily, Campbell took a step forwards but the blade touched Charmian's white neck cutting the delicate skin and drawing blood.

Sir Geoffrey put a warning hand upon his son's arm. 'Deane will kill her,' he murmured. 'They are desperate men. We have no choice but to let them go if—if we wish to spare Charmian's life.' There was a catch in the elder man's voice, so wrought with emotion. He had left his love, Elizabeth, injured, most probably fatally for all he knew, by her callous husband, to follow the escaped prisoners only to be forced to watch that same man now allow his daughter's life to be used as blackmail. Sir Geoffrey was no coward. He had seen fighting, had served his royal master through years of hardship, even torture, with a tenacious loyalty and a ferocious bravery, but never had he witnessed anything so despicable as the enemy he now faced, a man who would sacrifice the lives of his own wife and daughter to save his own skin.

'Let them go,' he said tiredly to Campbell.

'For the moment only, then,' Campbell muttered between his teeth. 'But he shall not escape my sword for long. I shall follow wheresoe'er he goes until I have my Charmian safe from his wickedness.'

With infinite tenderness the older man laid his hand upon the younger's shoulder. 'My son, take care, take care indeed for I fear for the dear child's safety.'

Helplessly, Sir Geoffrey and Campbell Denholm were obliged to stand and watch whilst Joseph Radley and the Deanes bore Charmian away. She gave one last despairing, anguished cry, 'Campbell!' which tore the young man's heart to shreds, but he dared give no sign, make no gesture towards her, lest her father should carry out his terrible threat.

So Charmian was carried away believing that Campbell could not forgive her, did not even wish to help her.

Charmian Radley bowed her head and wept.

Chapter Eight

They returned to Boston, but it was to a very different place from what they had believed their home town to be. With the promise of the restoration of the monarch, the Parliamentarians had been utterly routed. Alderman Radley was a powerful voice in the affairs of the town no longer and General Radley now had no troops at his command. All his one time friends and colleagues had either fled or had been arrested.

It could only be a matter of time before the Royalists came looking for Joseph Radley for he was regarded as one of the regicides. For him there would be no royal pardon, not even exile. For him there would only be death at the block.

Even their own home was no longer safe. The servants who had remained behind had now gone and the place had been broken into and looted. The furniture had been smashed, their belongings scattered, their Puritan garments ripped to shreds and hung grotesquely from the walls as an ominous threat of what treatment their owners might expect. As they walked through the echoing chambers, the vein in Joseph Radley's temple throbbed.

'Cowards! Traitors all! Is there no one left we can trust?' He swung round to face William Deane. 'If we can but get to Holland, we would be safe. I have business associates in Leiden amongst the cloth-makers there. They might help us to escape, eventually to the New World.'

Deane's eyes glinted. 'A good notion, Radley. I have heard tell that Holland is a haven for all manner of refugees. Among the Calvanists we may find sanctuary for the time being, at least.'

Charmian and Timothy Deane stood close beside each other listening to their elders discuss what was to become of them.

'Holland it is, then. But how to get there?'

'Boat?' suggested Deane. 'If there is Dutch shipping in the port of Boston, might we not find help there?'

' 'Tis a chance we will have to take.'

They found a sailing boat to take them to Holland though evidently it took all the money that Joseph Radley and William Deane possessed between them to bribe the master to take the fleeing Puritans aboard his vessel.

The wind howled along the deserted quay. The night was black and hid the four stealthy figures as they embarked. Behind them Charmian heard a movement and turned see the black-coated figure of a man step back and merge into the shadows. Was it a King's man come to arrest them at the very moment of their escape? The poor confused girl did not know what to hope for. Capture now would mean certain death for her father and the Deanes. And yet—she longed with all her heart to be safe back with her mother, to have the time to beg forgiveness from Sir Geoffrey and—if he would listen to her—from Campbell too.

But the shadows remained still and silent as her father pulled her aboard the foreign boat and Charmian believed that perhaps she had imagined that she had seen someone standing there.

They landed on the west coast of Holland on a lonely stretch of beach and made their way on foot to The Hague and thence to Leiden. Footsore and weary, their clothes stained by salt water, cold and hungry, they reached the outskirts of the town.

'Where do these friends of yours live?' William Deane asked of Joseph Radley.

'How should I know? I have never been here before. All I do know is that Johan Vermeer is a burgomaster of Leiden besides being a clothier.'

William Deane said, 'It should not be difficult to find his home then. Why do we not ask someone?'

Joseph Radley turned upon him. 'Ask someone? Ask someone?' he almost shouted. 'And risk being found out.'

'We are safe in Holland now, Radley. There are not Cavaliers lurking behind every tree here.'

Joseph Radley cast a wary glance behind him. 'Perhaps not, perhaps not. And yet I have the strangest feeling . . .' Brusquely he shook himself and said, 'Come along, if we are to find shelter before another nightfall.'

Charmian followed, clinging to Timothy Deane's arm. The two youngsters had drawn closer in the fear they shared and Timothy had found a new strength in his role as protector of Charmian.

'Courage, Charmian,' he whispered as his brother and Joseph Radley strode on ahead. 'It cannot be far now.'

'Oh Timothy,' Charmian said, tears ever close. 'I scarcely think I can go another step. May I not rest awhile?'

'Come along, come along,' her father's voice commanded making any respite impossible.

As they approached Leiden, they saw that the town still had a deep moat, but the walls and ramparts which had once been its protection had fallen into neglect and had become grassy banks with bushes and shrubs growing amongst the brickwork. Even the gate in the ramparts through which they passed to enter the town itself was no longer the guardian of the town it had once been.

The town of Leiden had been carefully planned with its almost circular street-plan and near the centre a tower housing the clock rose above the other buildings proclaiming the place which was the centre of the commerce of the town.

'That's where we should go,' Joseph Radley pointed to the clock. 'That is where we are likely to find Vermeer.'

They passed through the main streets, recently paved by the commercially minded Dutch municipality, still feeling as if they walked in circles, every so often passing a hump-back bridge across the canal which was an integral part of every Dutch town. They came at last to the market-place—the centre of the town life. Here people hurried about their daily work, and cries from the vendors filled the air, and scarcely a glance was directed at the four bedraggled strangers who moved slowly in bewilderment through their midst.

They were directed to the home of Johan Vermeer just off the market-place. It was a newly-built house in brick with four storeys proclaiming the wealth and importance of the owner. They entered directly from the street. Above them, at first-floor level, a canopy ran across the front of the house. Then came a series of windows, the surrounding casements decorated with light sandstone. On the third storey there were fewer windows and then above that the roof commenced and the much smaller fourth storey was set into the eaves.

They entered the house through a heavy oak door and found themselves in a well-lit entrance hall which led into a corridor with ante-rooms leading off it. They followed the house-servant as he led them towards a spiral staircase and into a reception room above. The room was furnished with walnut tables and chairs which shone, but dominating everything was a massive carved cupboard, the symbol that the home was that of a prosperous clothing merchant and burgomaster of Leiden for it displayed plates and pots and dishes—such possessions that would be unknown in a poorer household.

'Joseph Radley! This is a surprise. It is usually I who visit you, is it not, in Boston?' Johan Vermeer was a huge, beaming, welcoming man who scarcely showed surprise at their sudden arrival in his home or at their dishevelled appearance. He bade them join him at his meal and only then did he gently probe as to how and why they came to be here in Holland, in Leiden.

The burgomaster's house was elegant and charming, the dark wood of the doors and stairs shone rich and warm, whilst tapestries covered the cold walls. The floor of this reception room was paved with marble and the leaded windows sparkled.

The mistress of the house came into the room to greet her husband's guests with a quiet courtesy and stayed to listen to the story Joseph Radley had to tell. She was dressed in a dark violet gown over several petticoats. She wore a broad white collar and cuffs—a style so like her own puritan dress that Charmian almost gasped aloud in surprise, but as the burgomaster's wife came closer, Charmian could see that the quality of the cloth and the lace trimming on the collar and cuffs was very different to the coarse cloth Joseph Radley had obliged his wife and daughter to wear.

At the thought of her dear mother, tears welled in the girl's eyes, but no one seemed to notice for they were intent upon Joseph Radley's story.

'We have been driven from our homes by the Royalists,' Charmian heard her father begin. 'Our leader—our Protector—is dead, but you know that, of course. Since his death our cause has crumbled and the Royalists have brought back their King.' He thumped the table making the fine tableware jump and clatter.

'My enemy—one Geoffrey Denholm, God rot his soul—held me captive and sought to—to defile my wife and daughter while he kept me prisoner.'

Charmian gasped and turned white, but warningly Timothy put his hand upon her arm and she remained silent listening with growing terror to the lies her father was telling these good people.

'Even now I may have left my dear wife dying at the hands of that evil blackguard. Vermeer, I knew of nowhere to go save here, to Holland, in the hope that you may help us to escape eventually to America to follow in the footsteps of the first Pilgrims. Vermeer, we are at your mercy.' Joseph Radley spread his hands wide imploring his friend to aid them in their desperate situation. Never in her young life had Charmian seen her father put on such an act. Or had she? Had he not gulled her in exactly the same way into helping them to escape from the dungeons of Gartree Castle.

Charmian's head dropped forward and she closed her eyes. She was filled with shame and remorse and disillusionment as she listened to her father's lies and deceit. She was now as much his prisoner in this strange land as he had been in Sir Geoffrey Denholm's keeping, and, it seemed, in as much danger.

The burgomaster was speaking. 'Though you and I have enjoyed a good business friendship, Radley, over the years, and during the rule of the Commonwealth there was peace between our nations, yet there are many who still remember the Anglo-Dutch War of seven years ago, and believe that the present peace is now very uncertain. To please the new King of England they may feel it their duty to hand you over ...' He paused whilst Radley began to bluster again. 'Are you saying that *you* ...?'

'No, no, indeed not.' The Dutchman spoke English with perfect ease. 'But I think a long term stay here inadvisable. I think you should seek passage to the Americas as soon as it may be arranged. Meanwhile, I think the young ones,' he smiled briefly towards Charmian and Timothy Deane, 'would be better hidden if they lived with some of my workers, and perhaps we could even find them employment at a loom.'

Radley nodded. He would agree to anything the burgomaster suggested if it would save his own life.

'Possibly,' Vermeer added, 'the girl would be better protected dressed as a boy. But enough for this day. Tonight, you shall rest and tomorrow we shall make plans. Now, let us eat.'

They were shown into a room at the rear of the house where the entire household sat down to the meal. Johan Vermeer at the head and at the opposite end the children and the servants. Hesitantly, Charmian seated herself next to Timothy, quite unsure whether she was to be treated as an adult or as a child.

The table seemed laden with a vast variety of pots and dishes, sugar bowls, tureens, glasses and tall pewter mugs—such a rich variety which Charmian had never before seen. The midday meal was the most important of the four meals of a Dutch household: vegetable soup, fish and meat with a salad and then a dessert of pancakes which Charmian refused feeling she could not eat another mouthful. No wonder the burgomaster and his wife were rotund. Yet they were kindly and the warm, merry atmosphere of their family life enveloped Charmian, showing stark comparison to the harsh, stern life in her father's household.

Yet another light meal was enjoyed mid-afternoon and then the evening meal again resembled the midday, comprising several courses.

'Now, my little one.' The burgomaster was speaking to Charmian directly in his well-pronounced English. You look so tired. The girl

73

will show you to your room and, tomorrow, we will plan your new life.'

He spoke with great compassion as if he was thinking he was about to help this pretty English maid to escape the clutches of the wicked Cavaliers when in truth all Charmian longed for was to be back with her mother and Sir Geoffrey Denholm.

And with Campbell.

Chapter Nine

Charmian followed the Dutch maidservant up the twisting staircase to the upper floor. As she stepped into the bedroom she almost cried out aloud with surprise. After the sparsely furnished bedchambers she had occupied in her father's house and then the cold, forbidding vastness of Gartree Castle, this guest-room in the home of these kindly Dutch folk seemed luxury indeed.

Charmian felt the tears prick her eyelids. If only her dear, gentle mother were here safe and well, to share this comfort, to lie on the vast four-poster bed, so high that it needed a set of steps to climb into it and so broad that it took up a quarter of the space of the whole room. The damask bedspread had been folded back invitingly to reveal delicate embroidery upon the top sheet and the whole bed was surrounded by a green damask curtain. The walls of the bedroom were decorated with porcelain plaques and here and there a picture. A washstand was set at one side of the room with a basin and a jug of water upon its flat slab. Two low chairs and a linen cupboard completed the furnishings.

In but a few moments Charmian was sinking into the soft down of the feather-bag and, exhausted, she slept. Not even the night-watchman's whirling rattle and his lilting voice chanting the darkness away every hour disturbed her.

Yet the household was astir early and all the burgomaster's family were awake and dressed by the time the milkman cried, 'Warm milk! Sweet milk!' outside the windows.

Charmian opened her eyes, loath to leave the warm safety of the bed but at that moment the burgomaster's wife appeared, smiling and chattering to Charmian even though the girl could not understand a word she said. The Dutchwoman held a bundle of clothing in her arms, boy's clothing, and she gestured that Charmian should rise and dress herself. Amid these strange people, this unfamiliar language, for of the whole household only the burgomaster himself spoke good English, Charmian was obliged to submit to having her golden hair cut short, and her gown—drab though it might be—exchanged for the clothing worn by a young Dutch boy: trousers reaching just below her knees, a rough shirt and a jerkin.

'Shoes?' she asked the burgomaster's wife and pointed to her bare feet. The Dutchwoman smiled but shook her head and said something in Dutch and then gave Charmian a little push towards the door. Obviously, no shoes.

Charmian looked down at herself and tugged wistfully at her shorn hair. She looked just like a ragamuffin boy. The loose shirt and jerkin concealed her womanly shape and denied her femininity and when she found Timothy Deane waiting outside for her, dressed in a similar manner, Charmian felt fear wash over her. What was to happen to them? Tears welled in her eyes and she clung to Timothy's arm for support and comfort.

'I will take care of you, Charmian, I promise. I will not let them part us.'

'Oh Timothy,' she whispered. 'I am so afraid.'

They left the home of the burgomaster without even a farewell from Chairmian's father or William Deane. As they went beyond the gate and into the street and turned towards the town where the workers' cottages stood, close-packed together, Charmian glanced over her shoulder back towards the house they were being forced to leave. Although it was the home of strangers, she had felt safe, almost welcome, within its walls.

Beside one of the trees near the gate, half-hidden beneath the low branches stood a man in a black cloak. Charmian gasped and turned to Timothy. 'Look, oh look, there he is again.'

But by the time she looked back yet again, there was no black-cloaked figure beneath the tree. Charmian felt a stab of disappointment and once more wondered if her imagination were playing fanciful tricks upon her.

Sadly, she followed Timothy and the manservant who was guiding them to their new lodgings. Once more she glanced back, hoping to see the man again. He had seemed like a guardian angel to the frightened girl, not—strangely—a figure of menace.

But the vision had disappeared and Charmian felt more alone than ever.

They were passing into a poorer part of the otherwise thriving town. Here the streets were not paved. The ancient wooden houses overhung the roadway, the upper storeys leaning, almost drunkenly, towards each other.

They entered one of the houses, Charmian clinging to Timothy's arm. The inside was dark and musty and reeked of stale food, and human sweat. Seven families occupied the dwelling, each crowding into their own small allotted area for the house had been partitioned into as many apartments as the landlord could create. The place swarmed with children. Their voices filled the air, crying babes, yelling infants and shouting youngsters. Never had Charmian seen so many children. They scuttled from every corner to stare at her, to touch her boyish garments, whilst amidst it all the mother of the brood calmly spooned curds into the open mouth of her youngest offspring.

The woman nodded towards them and smiled and spoke in her own tongue, not a word of which Charmian could understand, though Timothy replied a little uncertainly in Flemish and pushed Charmian forward. He continued to speak to the woman and Charmian caught the mention of her new name, 'Pieter'. The woman finished her task and laid the infant in a wicker cradle.

A small, barefoot boy pushed past Charmian carrying a basket of wood. It seemed as if all the living was done in this one space, for in one corner, curtained off was a double bed—if bed it could be called for it was little more than a straw litter. In the opposite corner was a rough ladder leading to a loft above. No doubt that would be where she and Timothy would have to sleep alongside all these children.

Charmian and Timothy were put to work on a handloom amidst the clatter of a dozen such machines. The work was hard for the girl who had been sheltered and protected by her father's position. Now her father had lost his position and had been hounded out of his own land as a traitor. Already her feet were blistered and sore and now her fingers were chafed and cut by the threads. All about her the noise battered at her ears, the people shouted in a language she could not understand and even Timothy had been dragged away from her and obliged to work in another area. And every hour the church bells rang out, across the town, peal after peal, until Charmian almost dreaded the sound in her ears.

She missed Timothy's company during the day and at night when they returned to the small room overrun with children there was little time for sharing a few moments' conversation, a touch of the hands for comfort, for the Dutch housewife demanded yet more work from them: chopping wood, sweeping the one crowded room, minding the children, but when Timothy protested on Charmian's—Pieter's—behalf, it only seemed to make the housewife more impatient. By the time they climbed the ladder to the loft together, both Timothy and Charmian were too weary to do anything but fall on to their makeshift bed and sleep and sleep until rough hands shook them awake once more to a day of drudgery.

'Can we not run away?' Charmian whispered to Timothy. 'One night, could we not escape from here and find a boat to take us back to England?'

'We should never get beyond the town's gate-keeper, or we should be arrested by the night-guards patrolling the town.'

'Could we not leave before they come on duty at ten?'

Sadly Timothy shook his head. 'We should be missed here and they would send word to your father at once—you know they would. I don't doubt they are being well paid for having us in this—this hovel.'

Tears rolled down Charmian's cheeks. 'But I am so weary. Every bone in my body seems to ache and look at my fingers—they're raw and bleeding. And it hurts!' she ended pitifully.

'I know, I know,' Timothy tried to comfort her. 'Perhaps 'twill not be for very much longer. Perhaps even now your father is arranging for our passage to America where we will be safe.'

The tears only rolled faster. 'I—I don't want to leave England. I want to go back. I fear for my mother, I . . .' Unable to voice the terrible anxiety in her heart, Charmian fell silent. Timothy, too, could think of nothing to say, but shyly he put his arm about her shoulders and they sat together in the stale darkness of the room listening to the snorings and mutterings of the other occupants of this awful place.

Perhaps they might have gone on this way for days and weeks with Charmian growing more pale and tired, with dark blue shadows beneath her eyes and her once smooth hands torn and bleeding had something not happened which ended their life amongst the Dutch people with a brutal and frightening suddenness.

Perhaps—if they had been allowed to stay together—it would never have happened. But their enforced separation made Charmian long for Timothy's company all the more. Throughout the long working day, after Timothy had been taken away to work at a different loom, Charmian was surrounded by strangers, unable to communicate because she knew no word of Dutch and most of the time in trouble because she could not do the work correctly. Every moment she could escape, she crept away to meet Timothy in a corner of the yard behind their place of work. And that was where they were found one afternoon, only two weeks after they had started working, by an irate overseer who had come searching for them after finding their looms standing idle.

When the Dutchman saw them—to his eyes two boys—the one with his head upon the other's shoulder and the taller one with his arms around the golden-haired boy, the overseer lunged towards them shouting and brandishing his whip. The young pair sprang apart in horror, Timothy turning white as he understood the words the man was shouting at them. The overseer raised his whip and slashed Timothy across the face. Charmian screamed and threw herself against Timothy as if to try to shield him herself, but this only seemed to incense the man even more.

'No—no,' Timothy tried to explain. 'You don't understand. She's a girl—not a boy. We are doing nothing wrong.' But Timothy's Flemish was not good enough to explain such a complicated matter, though he could understand the filthy names the overseer was calling them both. Two more workers arrived and, listening only to what the overseer had to say, they grabbed hold of Timothy and Charmian and dragged them from the yard, through the workshops and out into the market-square. All the workers left their looms and followed, forming a ring around the accused pair, and as word passed amongst the onlookers, there was a murmuring amongst them which grew in a crescendo until the crowd were shouting and shaking their fists at the two young boys.

'Brand them. Brand the English dogs!' came the call, all their hatred of the English for the war not long forgotten bubbling to the surface.

Timothy cried out, 'No—no, not Charmian!'

But no one would listen. They did not even hear him.

On the corner of the market-square—unseen by the shouting, angry mob—stood a black-cloaked figure, his arms folded, his hat pulled low to conceal his face.

The man watched and waited.

The whole mass of people surged forward, screaming and shouting abuse, and Timothy and Charmian were lifted above their heads and tossed from one to the other, vile hands clawing and scrabbling and pinching. They were carried to one side of the square towards a blacksmith's where the overseer who had begun it all grabbed one of the irons hanging from the wall and thrust it into the red glowing coals of the blacksmith's brazier.

'That one first!' The overseer shouted pointing his whip at Timothy, whilst strong hands held Charmian captive.

She was forced to watch whilst Timothy's clothes were torn from his back leaving his skin white and vulnerable. They tied his hands behind his back and forced him to his knees. With relish the overseer pulled the branding iron from the fire and holding it before him, the end red and glowing, he advanced towards the cowering young man.

'Timothy—no—no—Timothy!' Charmian's shrill cry of anguish was heard even above the noise of the mob.

From the shadows the black-cloaked figure emerged, his right hand upon his sword hidden beneath the voluminous cloak. He moved towards the crowd. The branding iron came close to Timothy's shoulder, hovered and then plunged towards the pale, trembling, unmarked skin.

Timothy's cry of searing pain and Charmian's scream rang out together. There was the smell of burning flesh and a roar from the bloodthirsty crowd as the branding iron was removed leaving an ugly, raw scar on the young man's shoulder.

'Now this one,' came the cry as Charmian was dragged forward. She struggled but in vain, finding herself thrown to her knees on the cobbles. Someone removed the jerkin and then took hold of the thin shirt. The man in the cloak shouldered his way through the crowd.

Charmian closed her eyes in shame as the garment was ripped from her with one violent tug. Feeling the cool air on her sweating skin, she trembled a she waited for the branding iron to touch her back. She waited and then, strangely, she became aware of the silence about her. She opened her eyes. The crowd were staring at her, gaping at her smooth skin, her firm young breasts and seeing her now for the first time for the young woman she was, divested of her boyish garb. There was shame now on their faces and a shuffling of feet and a murmuring. The glowing branding iron fell to the cobbles with a clanging sound as the overseer saw his dreadful mistake.

Silent now, the crowd parted to allow the angry man from the shadows to move through them. As he came to the centre, he threw off his broad-brimmed hat and took off his cloak and wrapped it around the shivering, terrified and humiliated girl. Then he picked her up in his arms and carried her back the way he had come without speaking a word to the overseer or to the crowd, or even to Timothy Deane. He carried her towards his horse waiting in the shadows. Tenderly he lifted the girl up and sprang up behind her.

Only then did Charmian realize just who her rescuer was.

Campbell Denholm.

Chapter Ten

'How—how did you find me?'

They were at a small inn on the outskirts of Leiden. Charmian was sitting wrapped in a robe in a small bedchamber before a blazing log fire, whilst, at Campbell's command, the landlord's wife hurried to find some suitable clothes for her unexpected guest. They were alone in the room. Campbell stood looking down at her. Gently he reached out and touched the shorn locks of her golden hair, the hair he had loved so much.

'My Princess Golden Hair,' he murmured. 'What have those barbarians done to you?' He spoke not of the Dutch people who had treated her with a rough kindness until this tragic misunderstanding, but of her father who had used his daughter so cruelly. The tenderness in Campbell's tone threatened to overwhelm Charmian when she recalled what would have happened had he not appeared—so miraculously it seemed to her—at that very moment. Then she asked him, 'How did you find me? And—and my dear mother, how—how is she?'

'I have been close by you all the time you have been in Holland. There was a nasty moment when you embarked in Boston. I feared I would not find another boat quickly enough to follow you, for I had no idea then where your father intended to seek refuge. Luckily for me, your father has a great many enemies in Boston now and word came swiftly to my ears that he was bound for Leiden. The rest was easy. My men have gone to arrest your father and the Deanes at this moment though "arrest" is not quite the right term. Kidnap would—perhaps be a more appropriate word.'

The smile, once so readily leaping into his eyes, merely twisted his mouth with wry humour.

'Campbell—I know you must hate my father and the Deanes and—and I know what you must think of me after—after . . .' Her voice died away and she avoided his gaze. Campbell said nothing. 'But—but I beg you do not be too hard on Timothy Deane. He tried to protect me, he . . .'

'He did not succeed very well,' Campbell said curtly.

'I know it must look like that to you, but he was led by his brother, just as I was deceived by my father.' Charmian hung her head and so she did not see the anguish, the jealousy, in Campbell's eyes as she pleaded for leniency for Timothy Deane.

He moved away from her and said brusquely, 'I will see what I can do.' Then he added more gently and with a hint of sadness in his tone, 'But firstly, I must take you home as soon as I can. I shall not wait for my men to bring your—the prisoners. I can trust them to carry out my orders. You and I shall travel on horseback by road. The Dutch much prefer travel by canal and by avoiding the canals we may yet escape.'

'Escape? You mean we are not safe yet?' she asked in surprise. Campbell's mouth, once so gentle and smiling, was now so tight and hard. 'There are no laws of extradition between our countries and the only way for me to retake my prisoners is to spirit them away by night.'

So—she was his prisoner. That was how Campbell thought of her—as the enemy of his King.

As he made to leave the room, she cried, 'You have not yet told me of my mother.'

He paused, stood very still for a moment and then slowly he turned to face her. 'She is very ill. She was gravely injured by your father's horse. She—she lives only to hear news of you.'

Charmian's face was ashen. 'You mean she . . .' She could not voice the words, but Campbell knew their meaning and silently he nodded.

There was nothing he could say to comfort the girl though he ached to take her into his embrace and hold her close.

As it was, he turned away and left her alone with her grief and remorse.

The horses clattered to a halt in the cobbled courtyard—they were back at Gartree Castle. Campbell dismounted and held up his arms to help Charmian. Stiffly, she slid from her mount into his arms. But as soon as she was standing on the ground Campbell let go of her and moved away, without even looking at her. Charmian, her heart thudding with apprehension of what she was about to find within the castle, nevertheless picked up her skirts and ran towards the door that led into the great hall. From a chair by the fire a figure rose to greet her. With a cry of relief she ran forward. 'Sir Geoffrey, how is my mother? Please tell me at once.' She stopped and bit hard upon her lip, all her guilt flooding back at once. 'Oh—and you are hurt.' The shame washed over her yet again as she remembered her part in the terrible affair. But Sir Geoffrey was smiling at her, holding out one arm towards her. The other arm was supported in a sling.

'Only bruised, my dear,' he said quietly. 'Are you all right? They have not—harmed you?'

Dumbly Charmian shook her head, then in a low whisper said, 'Though I should have been badly burned—branded—if it had not been for Campbell. But—my mother?'

She felt the pressure of Sir Geoffrey's fingers upon her shoulder. 'My dear, the horses' hooves came down heavily upon your mother as she lay upon the ground.' His face was grey with anguish. 'I am afraid she was—is very badly hurt. I—I cannot but say that she . . .'

He faltered and Charmian stared up at him, realizing in that brief moment that his heartache was as deep as her own. 'You mean she is going to—to—die?'

Slowly, sadly, Sir Geoffrey nodded.

Charmian buried her face against his chest and sobbed, 'It is all my fault!'

'No, no, my dear child, you must not blame yourself. I shall not let you do so,' he said soothingly, stroking her short hair gently. 'You cannot be blamed for trusting your own father.'

Her voice muffled against him, Charmian said, 'I truly believed that he meant to swear allegiance to His Majesty. It—it was not until we—he so misused my mother, that I began to see how he had deceived me. Oh how cleverly he had deceived me,' she cried bitterly. 'I can never expect forgiveness. Sir Geoffrey, for I can never forgive myself.'

'We all understand, my dear little one. There is nothing to forgive in your actions. You have been so sheltered and protected—how could you ever recognize such wickedness?'

But Charmian could not herself believe his kindly words. 'Campbell will never forgive me,' she murmured unhappily.

Sir Geoffrey sighed and then he put his uninjured arm gently around her shoulders. 'Come, my dear, I will take you to your mother.'

When she entered the chamber where her mother lay, Charmian was surprised to see Lady Denholm seated beside the bed, holding Elizabeth's limp hand. Seeing her husband and Charmian, she rose and came towards the girl holding out both her hands to take hers, her voice full of sympathy. 'My dear girl. May the Lord be praised that you are safe.'

'How is she?' Charmian whispered afraid to hear the reply, yet ask she must.

'My dear. I am so very sorry, but—she has held on to life only to see you again, only to know that you are safe.'

Charmian bit her lips and tiptoed towards the bed. Her mother's face—still lovely—was deathly pale and her breathing was in short, painful rasps. Charmian gave a low moan and bent her head down to rest her cheek on her mother's hand. 'Oh Madam—my dearest mother—what have I done?'

Sir Geoffrey, standing at the opposite side of the bed, leant over. 'Elizabeth, my dear, Charmian is here. She is quite safe. Campbell found her and brought her home.'

Elizabeth Radley's eyelashes fluttered and opened and as Charmian raised her head she saw her mother try to smile. 'My darling

Charmian,' she whispered weakly and Charmian could see that even the effort to speak caused her great pain.

'No, Mother, don't try to speak. You must rest . . .'

'No, no, I must tell you, my love. You must not marry Joshua. Geoffrey—' she winced as she turned her head.

'I am here, my dear,' he said, gently taking her white, cold hand in his. All the while, Lady Denholm stood quietly at the end of the bed.

'Geoffrey,' Elizabeth whispered. 'Don't let Mary make her marry Joshua. Promise me!'

'I promise, Elizabeth. We will cherish Charmian as our own daughter.'

'You are so—good. And so is Georgina,' Elizabeth whispered. 'She is a wonderful woman to be so—so understanding. She has been so kind to me.'

Sir Geoffrey beckoned his wife closer and she too leant towards Elizabeth and spoke softly. 'We shall ensure Charmian's happiness, my dear Elizabeth. And keep her safe from those who would do her harm.'

'Charmian,' her mother whispered. 'Charmian—if he should ask you, you should marry Campbell. Remember—it is my wish that you should marry—Campbell. He—loves—you—so. Do you promise me, my dear daughter?'

'Oh, Madam.' The tears flowed down Charmian's cheeks, for she could not explain to her dying mother how Campbell, far from loving her, now despised her for what she had done. All she could whisper were the words, 'I promise.'

With that reassurance, Elizabeth Radley seemed to let go of her hold on life and quite quickly she slipped into unconsciousness from which she was never to recover.

For the next few days until well after her mother had been buried, Charmian stayed in her room, weeping inconsolably. In the afternoon of the second day after the burial, Lady Denholm came to sit with her.

'Now, my dear, your mother would not have wanted you to

grieve for her for too long. I know how sad and lonely you must feel. Your mother gone and your father—well—we are not quite sure what is to happen to him yet. But we want to take you home with us. Sir Geoffrey and I—and Campbell—want to take care of you as we promised your mother.'

There was a silence between them for some moments and then Charmian could no longer hold back the question that had, for so long, been in her mind. 'I—I do not understand you,' the words came tumbling out before she could stop them. You seem to bear my mother no ill-will, in fact, you have been most kind to her, and to me. And yet she—your husband—I mean . . .' she faltered, realizing at that last moment that she was trying to put into words matters which were perhaps better left unsaid.

But Lady Denholm was smiling wistfully. She took Charmian's hand in her own. 'My dear, I am not a jealous person by nature. I knew of Sir Geoffrey's love for your mother before I married him.'

Charmian's eyes widened. 'And you—you did not—I mean—did the knowledge of it not *hurt* you?'

Charmian knew how wounded she would feel, how fiercely angry too, if the man she loved were to love someone else.

Lady Denholm sighed. 'We have had a good marriage. There has been complete truthfulness and understanding between us always and a deep and lasting friendship. Sir Geoffrey is a fine man and I am honoured to be his wife. And we have our son of whom we are both so proud. And yet . . .' She paused and leant a little closer. You see, my dear, I understood so well because my heart had belonged to another.'

Charmian gasped and her lips parted in surprise. Lady Denholm nodded sadly. 'Sir Geoffrey and I were betrothed as children at our parents' insistence—just as you and Joshua Mason were. But that does not prevent one falling in love. I loved another man—a man my parents considered wholly unsuitable.' Tears welled in her eyes. 'I have never seen him during these last twenty-five years. I do not even know if he still lives.'

'But you—you have never forgotten him?'

'No,' Lady Denholm's voice was a mere whisper. 'No, I have never forgotten him.' More briskly, she added, 'So you see, Charmian, why I bear your mother no malice. I understand—oh so very well—how they both must feel. And,' she continued, squeezing Charmian's hand slightly, 'Sometimes we—all of us—must put duty before the desires of our own hearts.'

And now, because of her mother's deathbed wish, was Campbell to be made to marry her against the desires of his own heart?

Chapter Eleven

The following day, though Charmian was still pale and her eyes full of sadness, the storm of weeping had passed. She felt the need to escape from the confines of her room. So, putting on her warm cloak she left the castle and passed over the small footbridge over the moat and walked down the steep slope towards the river. From a narrow window, Campbell, a thoughtful frown on his face, watched her go.

The ground was hard and frosty, the trees naked of their leaves, the river grey and lifeless. How very different it all was from that sparkling autumn day she had spent with Campbell, laughing so joyously without a care. So long ago it seemed. How very different she felt now. Her sweet mother gone, and her father . . .

She shuddered. She tried not to think about her father. She did not know what to believe. She knew now that Campbell's men had, as he had put it, kidnapped her father and the Deanes and had brought them back to England. Now they waited in the Tower for His Majesty's decision.

And Campbell. Her mind shied away from thoughts of him too. How different he was from the merry young man he had been all those years ago.

She walked a short distance along the river bank and then her eyes caught sight of the arbour, nestling in the trees out of sight of the castle and she turned towards it. In the entrance, she paused. Here she had seen her mother and Sir Geoffrey meet.

Then she had not understood the depth of feeling between them. Now she realized how precious those moments must have been for them—two people desperately in love but forced by their parents' will to spend their lives apart.

The floor was covered with withered leaves and cobwebs hung from the roof, but Charmian sat down upon the seat and, pulling her cloak closely around her, she stayed there, rigidly motionless, watching the river until the cold seeped into her bones. But still she sat there, locked in her own misery.

It was there, a little while later, that Campbell found her—such a pathetic little waif, huddled into her cloak, that even his heart melted at the sight of her. He had watched her leave the castle, had seen her head bowed and her shoulders hunched and had known the grief she must be feeling. He had watched her disappear down the slope towards the river and then as the minutes had ticked away his anxiety had grown. He realized how lost and hurt she must be feeling and how he had done nothing to help her. Indeed he had only added to her humiliation and guilt.

Now he was worried. Surely she would not do anything foolish? Yet had not her actions in helping her father been foolish and unthinking? His own father, he knew, sympathised with her, but for himself, Campbell had been irritated by her naïveté. Now he began to feel that perhaps he had been too harsh. His years of exile had made him hard, he had experienced all manner of hardships whilst she had remained cloistered and protected and kept ignorant of life itself. She was not to blame, he saw that now.

He had prowled through the great rooms listening for the sounds of her return, always coming back to the windows overlooking the river. At last he could wait no longer and carelessly throwing his cloak round his shoulders he strode out and down the slope, almost running now in his eagerness to find her. He reached the river bank—there was no sign of her in either direction. Swallowing the fear that rose in his throat, Campbell ran a short distance along the bank and then retracted his steps and searched in the opposite direction. This way and that he scanned the river bank. He was about to call her name when he remembered the arbour and ran back towards it. As he approached it, he could see her sitting there.

Relief washed over him, and with it came an anger that she had made him feel so anxious.

'Charmian.'

She jumped up at the sound of his voice, startled out of her thoughts. 'Campbell! Oh—I . . .' Embarrassment coloured her face.

'What on earth do you think you are doing sitting out here in this freezing weather?' His harsh tone was like that of an anxious parent who vents his anger upon a wayward child. 'Do you want to catch pneumonia like your hero, Oliver Cromwell?'

'He is no hero of mine.' Charmian was stung to retort even through her grief.

'Really? Then why so keen always to help his followers?' His anger goaded her to show a defiance, yet it was not at all what she truly felt inside. 'You condemn me for having helped my own father?'

Campbell's lip curled disdainfully. 'Not if your father were following some worthwhile course, no, but . . .'

'It is only a difference of beliefs. Who is to say who is right or wrong?'

'I can see,' Campbell stepped menacingly nearer, 'that I shall have to teach you a lesson on obedience to your Sovereign, who reigns by divine right.' Before she could utter another word, he had swept her into his strong embrace and crushed her against him. She gasped as his fierceness forced the breath from her body. His mouth was upon hers, demandingly, bruisingly, forcing her mouth open. Then suddenly he was gentle, his hands caressing her, stroking her hair, his mouth tenderly touching her forehead, her eyelids, her cheeks and again her soft mouth searchingly. Wildly she felt an upsurge of emotion flood through her whole being once again. Just as before she had been powerless to resist him, now once more she found herself responding to his ardent kiss. Then she remembered his anger, his mockery of her, and she began to fight to free herself, telling herself that his embrace was loathsome to her, but her heart would not believe it.

'Let—me—go. How dare you?'

His laughter was a gentle breeze upon her face. 'I should enjoy teaching you to be a willing servant of the Royalist cause, my dear Charmian.'

'Never! Never! *Never!*' She flung herself from him and almost fell over backwards in her attempt to flee from him. 'Oh, I hate you. I *hate* you!' she sobbed and ran from the arbour, and up the slope towards the castle, running, running until her lungs were bursting. And all the time she could hear his mocking laughter in her ears.

That evening they dined in the great hall. Mary Mason, still mistress of Gartree Castle and yet a prisoner in it; her husband Edward, who was as silent and as unnoticeable as ever; Sir Geoffrey, his wife and son; Joshua, whose only interest in life seemed to be food—and Charmian. Charmian toyed with the food on her plate, her eyes downcast, her appetite gone.

'Sir Geoffrey,' she heard her Aunt Mason say. 'Arrangements must be made for the marriage between my son and my brother's child. You have no right to stop it any longer. It is time they were married and . . .'

Charmian raised her head and glanced towards her cousin, but he was too intent on stuffing more sweetmeats into his mouth to listen to the conversation going on over his head.

Sir Geoffrey cleared his throat. 'I promised Charmian's mother that I would see that she was not forced to marry Joshua.' His level gaze met Mary Mason's furious eyes. 'And I intend to keep that promise.'

As Mary Mason opened her mouth to speak, Campbell said, 'Exactly so. Charmian will marry me.'

For a moment there was a stunned silence around the table. Then Charmian gasped and stared wide-eyed at Campbell, whilst Mary Mason threw up her hands and gave way to hysteria. Joshua continued eating.

And Campbell—he met Charmian's horrified gaze with a mocking, half-bitter smile. 'Well, don't you want to be rescued from marriage to your cousin?' he asked quietly.

Mary Mason began to shriek. 'So, this is what you do in my

house, you vixen, you spurn my son and throw yourself at a damned Royalist. Aah, what will your father say, girl, what will he *say*?'

'Her father has no more say in her future,' Campbell snapped. 'He is the prisoner of the King and likely to lose his head.'

Charmian swallowed and slowly she stood up. With quiet dignity she faced them all. 'I do not wish to marry Joshua—or—or Campbell. I do not wish to marry anyone.' She made as if to leave the hall, but Campbell sprang to his feet, strode around the table and swept her up into his arms and carried her the length of the great hall, whilst she kicked and struggled but to no purpose.

'But I wish to marry you, Charmian, and your mother wished it. Did she not say—stop wriggling, will you?—did she not ask you that if I should propose, you should accept me? And did you not give her your promise?'

Immediately Charmian was still. She gave a low moan and put her hand across her face.

'So,' Campbell was saying sternly, 'that is all that is to be said.' He raised his voice and bellowed for Charmian's maid. 'Nell, *Nell* . . .'

Sir Geoffrey and his wife had followed Campbell to the far end of the great hall, leaving Mary Mason to her hysterics and Joshua to his eating. Edward Mason sat silently watching the whole proceeding with an expressionless face.

'Campbell,' his father said, a frown upon his face. 'What jest is this?'

Campbell turned to face his parents still carrying Charmian in his arms. 'No jest, Father, I do assure you. Charmian has the makings of a good Royalist wife and I intend to marry her.' He grinned at his father. 'Surely you do not object?'

'No—no,' Sir Geoffrey seemed for once utterly lost for words, 'but—but Charmian seemed to object—rather violently.'

His son laughed. 'Oh she will calm down and in time come to thank me for rescuing her from Joshua, won't you, my love?'

'Never! Never!'

'Ah Nell,' Campbell said as the maid appeared. 'Fetch your mistress's warm cloak and quickly put together a few things for her and ask Jem to make ready the coach. We are going on a journey.'

'What are you doing? Where are you taking her, Campbell?' Lady Denholm seemed as frightened of her son at this moment as Charmian was.

'To our home. To Ashleigh Manor. We shall be married there in our own chapel.'

'No, no,' Charmian began to scream and kick her heels.

'Campbell—think what you are doing,' his father began. 'Are you serious? Is this what you really want?'

Campbell's face was solemn. 'Oh I am very serious, Father, and yes, it is what I want.'

'Then I must insist you stop this nonsense and go about this in a proper manner. I promised her mother . . .'

'And Charmian promised her mother—did she not?—that if I were to ask her to marry me, she would do so?'

'Yes, but the child was put in an impossible position. Elizabeth was dying. She would never have extracted such a promise had she been well and—and . . .'

Gently Campbell said, 'I think Elizabeth Radley knew just what she was doing, Father. Don't concern yourself, I will take good care of Charmian.' And as he carried his reluctant bride from the great hall and out into the courtyard, he called back over his shoulder. 'The marriage will take place as soon as I can arrange it.'

He placed her in the coach and climbed in beside her. At once she began to struggle.

'Campbell, please, I beg you. Don't do this,' she began to sob.

'Thank you, Nell,' Campbell said calmly as the maid handed him Charmian's cloak. He wrapped it around her shoulders, which were shaking, not with cold but with fury. They waited, seated in the coach, whilst the horses were finally hitched and made ready. Sir Geoffrey's face appeared at the door of the coach. 'Campbell, your actions have displeased me. If you are making this child marry you against her will, just because of the promise she was obliged to give her poor mother, I shall not forgive you.'

Campbell returned his father's gaze steadily, unrepentantly. 'I am grieved to displease you, Father. But I promise you that one day Charmian will tell you herself that she is glad to be my wife.'

'I most certainly will not,' Charmian cut in. 'I would sooner marry Joshua than you.' But her tone lacked conviction. Once, long ago, she had told Campbell the exact opposite and now, suddenly, she remembered that very moment—that golden moment in the garden when as a child she had spoken from her heart without guile. 'Oh you're hateful!' She added now truculently and twisted herself finally from his grasp, but instead of attempting to get out of the coach she huddled in the corner, as far away from him as she could get and pouted moodily.

Campbell laughed. 'You see, Father. She is still a child in a woman's body. 'Tis time the woman in her was awakened and Joshua is not the man for that.'

His father smiled, suddenly seemed to relent. 'There I must agree with you, my son. But I beg you, please don't cause her anguish, I ...' But his words were lost to them, as Jem whipped up the horses and the coach was moving over the cobbled courtyard, out through the gates and over the drawbridge and down the hill towards the village.

Campbell sat back in his seat, spreading out his long legs and grinning insolently at her. Charmian refused to meet his gaze. She tried to tell herself that he was merely playing some foolish prank, at her expense, and that he did not seriously intend to go through with the marriage.

'How far is it to Ashleigh Manor?' she asked.

'Some distance, my dear. Several hours' drive—depending upon the state of the roads. We take a few hours' rest at an inn perhaps and journey on tomorrow. I hope you will love Ashleigh Manor as I do.' For a moment his expression grew softer as he talked about his home. 'It has fallen into disrepair during our absence, but it is a lovely house with parkland and gardens and a lake with swans,' he added impishly, reminding her of the happier times they had spent together. He leaned towards her in the darkness of the coach. 'Don't you remember, my princess, once saying that you wished it were me and not Joshua to whom you were betrothed?'

So, he had remembered too.

'Well? What if I did? I was only a child.'

'Ah, but a child always speaks the truth—didn't you know that?' Campbell mocked.

As the coach drew up before the main entrance of Ashleigh Manor late the following afternoon, servants seemed to appear from all directions.

'Welcome, young master,' was the chorus, beaming smiles upon their ruddy, jovial faces.

Campbell leapt from the coach and turned to give his hand to Charmian, but she refused his help and clambered down in an undignified manner. She felt, rather than saw—for she refused to look at him—Campbell's amusement at her petulant behaviour.

'Nell—take your mistress upstairs. You will be shown the way. See that she has everything she needs and that she rests now. It has been a long and tiring journey.' Then he caught hold of Charmian's hand and raised it to his lips. 'Until tomorrow, my love, when we shall be married.'

Charmian gasped and snatched her hand away. 'How much longer do you intend to carry on this ridiculous masquerade?' she snapped.

Campbell's face darkened and his mouth became a hard, uncompromising line. 'No masquerade, madam, I promise you. Tomorrow you shall become my wife!'

Charmian stared at him for a moment and then retorted, 'If you think that, then it is you who are mistaken, not I.' And with that, she flounced into the house and up the wide sweeping staircase to the bedchamber being hastily prepared for her. A huge log fire burned in the grate and food and drink were brought to her. She had never known such cosseting, such luxury particularly after the hard work and frightening experience she had suffered during her brief stay in a foreign land. Hot water was brought for her to bathe, fine silk garments—presumably Lady Denholm's—were laid out for her to wear. Idly she fingered the sheer nightgown.

'Oh miss,' Nell breathed, her young face red with excitement. 'Such a handsome husband you'll have and such lovely, lovely clothes. Oh miss, you'll keep me on as your maid, pray say you will?'

'Don't talk such nonsense, Nell. We shall not be staying here. Campbell Denholm is carrying on a cruel jape, that is all. There will be no marriage.'

'Oh miss, I think you are wrong. He has sent one of his men for the priest. And the chapel is being decorated with early spring flowers—snowdrops and crocuses and even a few daffodils, I think they have managed to find in the grounds.'

Charmian scoffed disbelievingly. 'Really, Nell, you would believe anything.'

'No, no. Miss, I saw it with me own eyes. One of the gardeners, he come in with armfuls of greenery and flowers—he knew just where to find them.'

Doubt began to creep into Charmian's mind. 'No, no, he does not mean it. He—he cannot!' she murmured, trying to convince herself.

'Come and bathe yourself, miss. Oh, there's such lovely perfumes here.'

An hour later Charmian was bathed and dressed in a silk bedgown and dressing robe in the palest pink. Nell was brushing her hair, still chattering excitedly. 'What a shame about your lovely hair all being cut off, but you will make the most beautiful bride still. Oh the bustling about that's going on below, you wouldn't believe it. They've even found Lady Denholm's own wedding gown. It was all so carefully wrapped away that it's as lovely as ever.'

'Nell, will you stop prattling about my marriage. There is not going to be any such ceremony.'

Tiredness was stealing over her. Warmed by the pleasant bath, she was sleepy and too weary to worry any more about Campbell's charade. She stretched luxuriously and yawned. 'I shall have to convince him in the morning.'

Within moments of snuggling down into the deep soft bed, she was asleep.

Chapter Twelve

Charmian awoke suddenly, not knowing where she was. Then she remembered. She had been abducted—there was no other word for it—and brought to Ashleigh Manor to become Campbell Denholm's wife. She smiled to herself. In the early morning light, the whole thing seemed even more ridiculous. She lay for a few moments and then got out of bed. In bare feet, she padded across the floor and opened the heavy door of her bedchamber.

'Good-morning, my love.'

She jumped as Campbell spoke from the shadows. He rose from a deep armchair and came towards her. Charmian gasped and her mouth fell open. 'What—what ever are you doing?'

'Guarding my future wife. Seeing that she does not attempt to flee from me.'

'You—you have been here, outside my door, all the night?' she asked wonderingly. Campbell noded slowly, his gaze never leaving her face. She stared at him, her last belief that this was all some wild jest falling away. He meant to marry her. Even against her will, he meant to take her.

As if reading her mind, he said quietly, 'You shall not escape me, Charmian. You are to be my wife—just as you promised your mother—and there is nothing you can do to prevent the marriage taking place.'

'I—I can refuse to speak the vows.'

For an instant anger flashed upon his face. 'But you won't, my dear.' It was a command rather than a request. Then Campbell laughed and in the face of his laughter, she felt her resolve to be of no consequence. His fingers reached out and touched golden hair, cropped short by the burgomaster's wife.

'How could anyone have done this to you?' he murmured, and then his eyes darkened with passion. 'Tonight, my love, until tonight.' His lips brushed her mouth softly and then he was gone, striding away down the long passage, raising his hand as if in farewell. 'Even the bridegroom must make himself ready, my love.'

Charmian slammed the door with all her strength and leant against it, breathing hard. Why, she told herself angrily, when I loathe him so much do I tremble at his kiss? Because, came the reply from deep within her soul, because you love him.

Why could she not agree happily to this marriage, for it was what she wanted most in all the world? Because, her heart answered, he does not love you. He is only marrying you out of duty to your mother's dying wish; to please your mother, whom his father loved. It was as if Campbell were trying to recompense for the lost love of Elizabeth and Sir Geoffrey, as if the union of their children would give them joy after the lonely years of their own separation.

Charmian closed her eyes and groaned aloud and sank to the floor. 'But if only he truly loved me,' she cried.

The servants at Ashleigh Manor were far more excited about the day's celebration than was their future young mistress.

' 'Twill be like the old days,' Charmian heard an older maidservant telling the younger girls. 'Before those damned Puritans stopped all our fun-making.'

'Ssh,' whispered another. 'The young miss—she's a Puritan.'

The older woman cackled with laughter. 'Not for long, she won't be. No pure maid after this night with our young master.' And she cackled raucously once more. The younger girl sighed dreamily. 'Oh, but she's the lucky one to be marrying the young master.'

About mid-morning, Sir Geoffrey and his wife arrived in time for Lady Denholm to inspect her wedding gown and pronounce it fitting for her daughter-in-law to wear. The white silk gown, with tight-fitting bodice and sleeves and its full skirt embroidered with gold, needed only the hem taken up a little, and Neil stitched and stitched with feverish excitement until her fingers were quite sore, whilst from every corner the bits and pieces believed to be so necessary by the merry-making Royalists appeared. Suddenly everyone was caught up in the whirl of a pre-Cromwellian celebration. Gloves, garters, scarves and ribbons, all adorned the bride, but it was not until after the ceremony that Charmian understood just why.

'My dear Charmian,' Lady Denholm took the girl's hands in her own. 'All this must be very strange for you, but pray be not afraid—Campbell will protect you. The servants have long been oppressed and their joy at being reunited with the Denholm family and the marriage of Campbell—their undoubted favourite—will lead them to celebrate in the only way they know how. It may seem very vulgar and bawdy to you, my dear child, but be assured they mean you no harm. They want to love you as we already do.'

Tears sprang unbidden to Charmian's eyes at the kindness in Lady Denholm's words. And whilst she knew that her father would disapprove most strongly of the day's happenings, deep in her heart Charmian knew that her mother would not have done so.

The marriage took place in the chapel of Ashleigh Manor at noon on a bright spring day. Campbell was resplendent in a dark blue silk doublet and breeches, with a velvet cloak trimmed with lace and lined with silk, his hair, at present longer than Charmian's, curling to his shoulders, his neat beard not quite hiding the scar on his cheek. His face was solemn as he watched Charmian walk slowly to meet him before the altar, his gaze steadfastly upon her pale face. She held herself rigidly erect as if she were merely obeying the wishes of her mother and yet she herself was determined to hold herself aloof and totally remote from the proceedings.

The words intoned by the priest and repeated mechanically, passed over Charmian's head '. . . to have and to hold . . . for richer, for poorer . . . from this time forward . . .'

Then, as it came to the words '. . . I plight thee my troth . . .' Charmian faltered. The words suddenly came to be the vow they represented. She was about to give herself wholly to Campbell for the rest of her life. Now Charmian hesitated.

The silence in the chapel lengthened and then the priest repeated the words more firmly, urging Charmian to say them, to make her vow. There was a restless murmur amongst those present as, slowly, Charmian turned her head to meet Campbell's steady gaze. His eyes were unreadable depths—she could not see the love there that she had hoped to find. Now—more than ever—Charmian was convinced that Campbell was marrying her only out of a sense of duty.

'My child,' the priest whispered, 'will you not make your vow?'

Charmian turned her gaze away from Campbell and looked towards the altar. The rich altar cloth and the ornate, bejewelled cross which had been hidden during Cromwell's rule had miraculously reappeared. The Royalists were rising again whilst her own father now waited in the Tower for certain death. And yet even as these thoughts flew through Charmian's mind, she seemed to hear her mother's dying voice. 'Remember—it is my wish that you should marry Campbell.'

Whatever lay behind Campbell's reason, Charmian's own was plain enough, she must fulfil her promise. She lifted her chin a little higher and the words came haltingly from her lips, '. . . I plight thee my troth.'

A sigh rippled through the chapel. It was done. They were married.

Almost before they left the solemnity of the chapel, the making merry began. Charmian was shocked and a little afraid as she found herself and Campbell surrounded by the laughing, jostling servants. Fingers reached out to pluck the ribbons and scarves from her dress. A manservant, bolder than the rest—made so by the ale he had already consumed in honour of the bridal pair—caught at the hem of her gown and made to lift her skirt.

'A garter, a garter from the bride!' he cried. Charmian gave a cry more of surprise than alarm, but at once Campbell's hand fastened upon the man's wrist. 'I claim sole right to that, my friend,' and whilst his tone was jocular, there was no mistaking the command.

The gaze of the master and his servant met for an instant and then they both laughed and the latter released his hold upon the bridal gown and gave a low exaggerated bow towards Campbell and his lady. 'Sire, I would deny thee not thy pleasure!'

Bawdy laughter broke out on all sides and Charmian felt it to be at her. Above the bobbing heads she caught sight of Sir Geoffrey and Lady Denholm standing a little apart from the mêlée, yet seeming to enjoy it all, seeming to condone this behaviour so strange to Charmian whose protected, well-ordered life had been so very different.

If the wedding had not been so hastily arranged there would have been a great number of invited guests—Royalists all—in attendance. As it was, apart from the bridal pair, there was only Sir Geoffrey and his wife and the members of their household present. Nevertheless, the procession from the chapel to the Manor and the waiting banquet was accompanied by a great deal of noise—music from lutes, fiddles, cymbals and drums, laughter, dancing and singing. Amidst it all, Campbell took his wife's hand and led her proudly towards the Manor, a broad smile upon his face.

In the great hall a magnificent feast had been laid out. How ever these good people had managed all this preparation in the space of one night, Charmian could not begin to imagine. All at once, she felt humbled by their kindness, by their obvious love for their young master and their ready approval of her as his wife.

His wife! She was now Campbell's wife.

All around her the noise and the laughter went on and on until late in the evening whilst Charmian, seated beside her husband, remained very quiet, eating little, her face pale with exhaustion.

Campbell leaned towards her. 'Am I so repugnant to you, Charmian,' he whispered, 'that you cannot even bring yourself to join in our wedding feast? Did you really prefer the odious Joshua?'

Charmian shook her head. At least she owed Campbell the truth. Almost inaudibly, she said, 'No—no, I did not wish to marry Joshua. I said that in anger—it was not true. But—but neither do I wish to spend my life with a man who despises me, just—just because of the wish of a dying woman.' She turned to face him now, looking directly into his brown eyes. 'Did you really think that you could make up for the lost love between your father and my mother? Did you imagine that by marrying me you could atone for their unhappiness?'

His dark gaze was upon her face, his eyes unreadable depths. Her voice shook a little as she turned from him, murmuring, 'I shall never forgive you for what you have done this day. Never!'

She rose, hoping to leave quietly and unobserved, but escape was impossible. As soon as she stood up the cry echoed around the vast room, 'The bride, the bride.'

As if it had been a signal, she was at once led away by six or eight laughing, chattering young women.

'The bedding, 'tis time for the bedding!' went up the exultant cry and Charmian glanced back to see a like number of young men advancing upon Campbell.

For the next hour, amidst much ribaldry, Charmian was obliged to submit to being disrobed and adorned in a fine linen bedgown.

'Where's all her hair-pins. We must leave no pins, 'twill bring ill-luck,' one young girl exclaimed. 'Oh madam—why ever is your hair so short?'

'It—was cut off—when I was in Holland.'

The young girl's eyes sparkled with interest. 'Was that when the young master rescued you?'

All at once the ugly scene in the market-place was vivid in Charmian's mind. The angry mob, the branding iron and Timothy's anguished cry of pain. With a surge of guilt, Charmian realized suddenly that over the last few days she had not once given thought to Timothy nor indeed to her father in the Tower.

She did not know for certain if they were still alive.

The girl was chattering on and her words interrupted Charmian's own thoughts. 'Were you ill-treated then, like Sir Geoffrey and Master Campbell in Spain? Oh treated bad, they were. They don't talk about it, but some say they was tortured by the Spanish for being spies. That's how Sir Geoffrey lost the use of his right arm, and how the young master got that scar. Mind you, I think it makes him all the more handsome.'

'Tortured? In Spain? I did not know of it.'

'Now, now,' put in an older woman, 'this is no talk for a wedding night. Stop your prattle, Mary Jane.'

'No, no, I want to hear it,' Charmian insisted. 'What happened in Spain to Campbell and Sir Geoffrey?'

'We don't know much more than that, madam,' the older woman now answered, 'all we know is that when Sir Geoffrey and Master Campbell were forced into exile, they fled to France and from there to Spain. But there's something happening there called the—the inquisition—and they were arrested and questioned and—we've heard tell—tortured. Oh, it has left its mark, and not only on the young master's face. He's not the merry young man he was. He's got a dark side to him now that he never had before. And Sir Geoffrey, why it's made an old man of him. But now, there's happier times ahead for us all now we've rid ourselves of these damned Puritans.'

Charmian was silent. How these people hated the Puritans and how they adored their own master and mistress. Charmian was lost, unable to decide what she should believe.

Who was right? Her father with his strictness, his harsh standard? Yet his faith and beliefs were sincere, she knew. Or the Royalists with their love of life and pleasure? And yet they too worshipped in their churches and made their pledges with a faith that was just as sincere. But this deep introspection was interrupted.

The time had come. Amidst much jollity, she was led towards the massive four-poster and then Campbell was ushered into the room by his male attendants and urged to climb into bed beside his bride.

But all was not done yet.

'Tell the priest we are ready for the blessing.'

A quietness fell upon the gathering as the priest who had married them entered the room to bless the marriage bed. That done, Charmian thought, they will all leave but still there were more customs the happy revellers remembered from the days before the Puritan rule.

'We must fling the stocking. Here, Mary Jane—see if you can do it.'

'I never heard of it. What must I do?' the young girl giggled.

'Stand here, at the end of the bed and throw the young mistress's stocking over your shoulder and see if you can hit her. If you do, 'twill be you next in the marriage bed!'

The girl squealed with delight and flung the stocking over her shoulder hitting Charmian full in the face.

The women laughed. 'You'll be the next to marry. Now young William—you try to do the same with the young master.'

It was obvious that Mary Jane and William were considered promised to each other and he, blushing red, performed the custom to the delight of all the women as Charmian's other stocking landed on Campbell's head, drooping comically over his nose.

'There, your fate is sealed, Master William,' Campbell teased. 'You cannot escape marriage to your Mary Jane now, for we have all witnessed that you are next to marry.'

The young man shyly put his arm about Mary Jane. 'Nor do I wish to escape, Master Campbell.'

'Now—off you go and my thanks for making this day possible.'

'One more thing before we leave, young master.' One of Campbell's attendants stepped forward holding a goblet. 'A posset of hot wine, milk, eggs, sugar and spices. 'Tis said to fortify the bridegroom and the sugar to make him kind.'

Unsparing of Charmian's blushes, the laughter rose again, as Campbell drank from the goblet.

At last the merry-makers departed, though their laughter could still be heard even through the heavy door. But in the bedchamber all was quiet and the darkness enveloped them.

Charmian felt Campbell move towards her, his arm slip around her, as she lay rigidly afraid now that the time was here.

'Charmian, oh Charmian,' he whispered close beside her. 'Do not be afraid. I would not hurt thee—never would I cause thee pain . . .'

When she awoke the following morning she was alone. As on the previous morning it took her a few moments to remember where she was and all that had happened on the previous day—and night.

Unbidden, a small smile curved her lips as she remembered. Campbell had soothed away her fears with unexpected tenderness. He had been demanding yet not brutal until in spite of her initial unwillingness, she found herself responding to him. Never had she imagined it would be like that. By the time he had taken her completely she had submitted to him readily, willingly and pleasurably, her love for him which she had tried so desperately to hide at last overflowing and engulfing her as she felt his need, his desire, for her.

Perhaps matters between the young couple might have gone on improving gradually, but Fate had another blow in store that threatened to tear them apart and to destroy the growing tenderness between them.

Campbell greeted her when she descended the stairs and entered the dining-room, an unfathomable expression upon his face once more. A little shyly, Charmian took her place at the opposite end of the long table. This morning she was hungry.

About half-way through their meal together, they heard a commotion in the hall. The door burst open and a young man dressed in the uniform of the Royalist soldier came running towards Campbell. 'Sire, sire.'

'Ah, Wentworth. You're back from London. What news?'

The man paused to catch his breath. 'Oh Master Campbell, 'tis grave. We took the three prisoners to London as you ordered. They are in the Tower, but not, I fear, safe. The Royalists refuse to wait for the King's return.' As the young man paused again for breath, Campbell looked up at him keenly, and Charmian stopped eating and waited for him to continue. 'They are lusting for blood and have taken matters upon themselves. They have condemned your prisoners—along with several others—to death. They go to the block the day after tomorrow.'

Charmian gave a little cry. 'Oh no! No!'

Campbell appeared to be deep in thought for a moment and then, to Charmian's distress, he quietly continued eating his breakfast. 'Thank you, Wentworth. You may go.'

'But, sire . . .'

'I said, you may go, Wentworth,' Campbell repeated firmly.

'Ay,' the young man muttered and left the room.

Charmian watched this man who was now her husband. Quietly she asked, 'Do you mean to let them die without even a proper trial, without even the word of His Majesty?'

'I cannot think,' he replied with deliberate calmness, 'that you can possibly have much affection for your father after the way he has treated you—and—your mother.'

'I—no, I suppose not, but he—he is still my father. If the King decrees he must die then—then so be it. But on the *King's* word and not at the hand of bloodthirsty Cavaliers.'

Campbell twirled the goblet set near him, his eyelids lowered hiding his eyes. The length of the table separated the two young people physically, but their beliefs, their differing backgrounds, were destroying their chance of happiness together. And then Charmian's next words finally cut that tenuous bond, sweeping away the lingering memory of their night of love in the morning's cold, harsh light of reality.

'What of Timothy Deane? He was led by his elder brother. He would not have been party to my abduction. He tried to care for me, protect me and . . .' She paused, breathing heavily, her bosom rising and falling, her eyes flashing.

'And what,' Campbell asked with deceptive languor, 'does Timothy Deane mean to you—exactly?'

'I do not understand your question. He—he helped me, he was kind to me . . .'

Campbell's head snapped up. 'Are you in love with him?'

Charmian gasped, wide-eyed. So that was it. Campbell was prepared to sit here and do nothing whilst his three prisoners were sent to their deaths just because of a belief that she—his wife—loved Timothy Deane.

When she did not answer his question, Campbell rose slowly, almost menacingly, to his feet and leant, his knuckles upon the table, towards her. 'Was that what you meant when you said you wanted to marry for love? Was that why you hesitated over your vows in the chapel? Was it the wrong man standing at your side?

Were you wishing for *Timothy Deane?*' As he spat out the name, he flung his chair to the side of the room and then with one violent movement, he upturned the table, the dishes and goblets, the food and drink, spilling on to the floor.

Terrified of his sudden rage, Charmian ran from the room. His outburst spent, Campbell listened to the sound of her feet flying up the stairs. He groaned aloud and for a moment covered his face with his hands. Last night he had begun to hope, but now, in one brief moment of jealous outrage, he had shattered those moments of tenderness perhaps for ever.

Then he raised himself. 'Wentworth! *Wentworth!*' he bellowed, and when the young soldier appeared, 'Give orders for my horse to be saddled. I must speak with my father and then we ride to London. But my wife is not to be told. She is to think only that I am on business about our estates. See to it.'

In her bedchamber—the bed still rumpled from their love-making of the previous night—Charmian paced the floor in a ferment of anger. How could he be so unfeeling, so obstinate?

Nell sidled into the room.

'Where is he, where is Campbell?' Charmian snapped at her.

The girl jumped then said, 'He's just ridden off, miss, I mean madam.' She giggled and then realizing her mistress was in no mood for humour, pulled her face straight. 'I'm told he has gone on business about the estates. Everything's in a turmoil, madam. Whilst him and his father . . .'

'Yes, yes,' Charmian waved her aside. 'Go away, Nell. I must think.'

As the door closed once more behind the girl and Charmian was left alone she began to scheme. So, she thought, he will go casually about his estate and leave men to die, will he? Well, she told herself, if he will not go to London, then I must. I am his wife now and daughter-in-law of Sir Geoffrey Denholm by marriage, am I not? Maybe there is something I can do.

'Nell, Nell,' she called now, 'send word to the stable for a horse to be saddled. I wish to—to go riding.'

Only the older, most trusted servants knew where Campbell had really gone. The rest, like Charmian, believed him to be riding about his own estate. So, the stable-boy believed that the young bride wished to follow her husband and ride with him, and swiftly he prepared a mount for her. No one except Nell and the stable-boy saw her leave. No one else saw her canter down the long drive leading from Ashleigh Manor, through the parkland, past the lake, past the deer grazing in the park and out of the boundaries of the estate.

Having asked the way, she was soon cantering steadily along the road to London, congratulating herself on her escape.

It was an hour or so later when one of the older grooms, who knew where Campbell had gone, learnt of his young mistress's departure.

'She's only gone in search of her 'usband,' the stable-boy told him and grinned cheekily.

'Maybe she has,' the elderly groom, Joby, replied. 'But she'll not find him! He's ridden to London!'

'Nay!' the stable-boy said. ' 'As he?'

'Ay,' the old man wrung his hands. 'We'd best send out looking for the young lady, else she'll be lost. Run to the Manor and see that Sir Geoffrey is told.'

By noon the men who had been out searching for Charmian returned one by one to the Manor house. Sir Geoffrey and Lady Denholm waited anxiously for news.

'We've scoured every part of the estate, sire,' a weary Joby reported. 'There is no sign of the young mistress, nor of her horse.'

'And you say she knew nothing of Campbell's journey to London?'

'No, sire. He was very firm. She was to be told only that he was out attending business of the estate.'

Sir Geoffrey pondered and then asked, 'Yet you say she heard all that Wentworth had to tell Campbell this morning?'

'So I believe, sire.'

'Then I am very much afraid,' Sir Geoffrey turned to his wife. 'That Charmian most probably believing that Campbell meant to do nothing to help her father, has tried to take matters upon herself. I fear she has set out for London.'

'Oh no! The child will be in such danger on the roads. And even if she should reach the city what can she hope to do? Nell,' Lady Denholm asked of Charmian's maid. 'How was your young mistress dressed when she left the house to go riding?'

Nell thought for a moment. 'In her old grey dress and black cloak, madam.'

'Oh Geoffrey,' Lady Denholm put her hand upon her husband's arm and her eyes were brimming with tears as she looked up at him. 'Charmian has gone amongst those bloodlusting Royalists in her Puritan dress!'

Briefly, Sir Geoffrey touched his wife's hand in a gesture of comfort. 'Then I must follow her at once.'

Chapter Thirteen

If it had not been for the urgency of her mission and for the anger in her heart against Campbell, Charmian would have enjoyed her morning ride towards London.

Spring was in the air. The cold frosts had gone and the hedgerows were giving promise of the new growth to come. Her horse was tiring, she knew, and she too was hungry. But in her hasty flight she had not thought to bring any coins with her. Sheltered and protected always, she had never needed to think of the necessity for such items.

There was an inn ahead and she decided to try her luck there. Perhaps Campbell's name was so well known that she would be served anyway. She rode into the inn yard and almost at once regretted her impulse.

Standing talking were three soldiers, Cavaliers all three. She tried to spur her horse to turn around, but one of them had already seen her and swiftly he ran forward and seized the bridle of her horse, making the animal rear dangerously. Desperately, Charmian clung on.

'Well, well, well. What have we here? A Puritan maid fleeing for her life? And alone too.'

'Leave go of my horse, sir. My name is—is Charmian Denholm. I am Campbell Denholm's wife.'

The man laughed and called out to his companions. 'Hear that, this wench says she's Denholm's wife. Now, I had not heard that he had married, had you?'

Their guffaws of laughter reached her ears. Another strolled over.

'Campbell Denholm married? Never in this world. Oh the ladies love him, but he slips their noose every time.'

Charmian held out her hand towards them, trying to still its trembling. 'There is his ring—see for yourself.'

But the handsome Cavalier's eyes were on her face. Suddenly he swept off his plumed hat and made a majestic bow. 'Of course, m'lady,' he winked at his companions. 'Whatever you say.' He was handsome but with insolent eyes, a long nose, and a small mouth which was hidden behind a moustache and pointed beard.

'What say we offer this lovely lady a ride in our coach—to wherever she is going, eh?'

The other two laughed heartily and agreed.

'My name is Anthony de Lisle,' continued the acknowledged leader of the group. He swept down in a low bow once more. 'I should be honoured if you would sup with me before we travel on.'

'I . . .'

'If you are worried because we are strangers, let me put your sweet head at ease. I—and my companions—are well acquainted with your—er—husband, Campbell Denholm.'

Charmian was still doubtful, but not only would it solve the problem of her impecunious state, but also her horse was extremely tired and really ought not to be ridden farther.

'Then I should be most grateful,' Charmian murmured, reassured by de Lisle's mention of Campbell's name as she allowed him to help her dismount.

As he ushered her inside the inn, de Lisle murmured to one of this friends, 'I did not think m'lady would succumb so easy!' And his friend laughed aloud.

Sir Geoffrey, in pursuit of Charmian, stopped at every inn on the road to London leading from Ashleigh Manor, but Charmian had a few hours' start ahead of him, whilst Campbell, ignorant of the danger his bride of but a few hours was now in, was already in London.

Charmian had enjoyed a meal of roast veal and now they were

in de Lisle's coach bowling along the highway towards the city. This coach was a deal more comfortable than her father's, Charmian thought, and the roads leading to London were better than the country lanes she was used to travelling upon.

'I wish to be taken to the place where the King will be,' Charmian said leaning forward. 'What do they call it—the Palace of Whitehall?'

'As far as we know His Majesty is not returned to London, yet, m'lady.' De Lisle's eyes mocked her.

'I know, but I wish to be waiting when he does return. There—there are people I must see there.'

Soon they were passing through the narrow streets of London. Open sewers ran down the side of the road and the houses overhung the road so that much of the light was shut out. The coach drew up before a terraced house in a better quarter of the city.

'This—this is not the Palace of Whitehall, is it?' Charmian observed shrewdly and met de Lisle's gaze squarely.

'I thought you would be far more comfortable at my town residence.' His eyes challenged her insolently.

'How dare you?' she raged, but suddenly she realized that she was helpless against the three of them. Fear began to creep over her, fear and a sense of shame at her own foolish impetuosity. How angry Campbell would be—and he would have every right! Yet, unbidden, came the thought that at this very moment she would have given anything for sight of him.

At first de Lisle was courtesy itself. His two companions left, with much chaffing and nodding and winking to de Lisle. He ushered Charmian up the steps and into his house. He was charming, courteous and attentive, and some of her fears were briefly allayed. He ordered refreshments for them and plied her with sweetmeats and wine and for over two hours he was a considerate host. But Charmian was agitated lest she should arrive too late to plead for the lives of her father and the Deanes.

They were due to go to the block within twenty-four hours, whether the King returned or not.

'Please, Master de Lisle, take me to the Palace of Whitehall. I must seek help on a most urgent matter.'

'Can it not wait until the King returns? Everything must wait until the King returns. And in the meantime . . .' His eyes glittered, and Charmian felt afraid again.

'No—no. This cannot wait. Some friends of mine have been wrongly arrested and—and condemned. I have come here to try to help them.'

'Ah,' de Lisle said, leaning back with a satisfied smile upon his face. 'Then you *are* a Puritan. I thought as much!'

'What I told you is the truth. I am Campbell Denholm's wife. But I am the daughter of a Puritan.'

She faced him resolutely and under her steady gaze, de Lisle's confidence seemed to falter and for the first time real doubt crept into his mind. 'If you are speaking the truth, then Denholm is like to kill me for what I have done.' Then he gave a short bark of laughter. 'No, no, 'tis not possible. Denholm married to a Puritan? In exile, he swore death to every Puritan that ever drew breath!' De Lisle leant towards her and made as if to grasp her in his arms. 'I cannot think that even a wench as pretty as you could make him break his oath.'

Charmian screamed and sprang up and tried to rush from the room, but de Lisle was to the door before her, barring the way.

Sir Geoffrey entered the fifth inn along the road to London.

'Have you seen a young lady riding on horseback pass this way, landlord?'

'Nay, sire,' the landlord said, 'I don't believe I have . . . What is it, boy?' he added impatiently as a stable-lad pulled at his sleeve.

'Sir, there was a young lady, she had a meal here with those three Cavaliers.'

'Aye, but the gentleman said she was alone, not with three others.'

'But she came alone. They stopped her in the yard, thinking she was a Puritan trying to escape.'

'Describe her to me, boy,' Sir Geoffrey demanded sharply.

'She was wearing a cloak, sir, a dark colour, but she had fair hair, gold, it was.'

'And you say she—she was with three men?'

'Ay, they took her off in their coach.'

Sir Geoffrey's face was dark with fury. 'Did you know them?'

'I knew the one who owned the coach. It had his crest on the side. It was Lord de Lisle.'

'My God—de Lisle,' muttered Sir Geoffrey, his hand automatically touching the hilt of his sword, 'that notorious scoundrel!'

He turned and hurried from the inn. 'Jem,' he shouted to his manservant accompanying him. 'Ride on to London—to the Palace of Whitehall. You can ride quicker than I now . . .'

Brusquely he brushed aside the cruel thought that once he would have been strong and fit enough to ride full speed all day. Now the years were forcing him to pass the task to a younger man. 'Find Campbell. Tell him that de Lisle has Charmian.'

The young man spurred his horse and clattered out of the inn yard, leaving Sir Geoffrey to remount and follow as quickly as he could.

The landlord, watching from the doorway, allowed himself a wry smile. 'I wouldn't be my Lord de Lisle when Master Campbell Denholm catches up with him!'

'Now, come on, my little beauty.' De Lisle was advancing towards her. 'You would not like me to hand you over to my friends, would you? They are intent upon seeing all Puritans at the end of a pike.' Charmian blanched and, keeping her eyes on him, moved backwards around the room. Frustrated passion glowed in de Lisle's eyes. 'Ah, so you want to make a game of it, my lovely, do you?'

'If you dare to touch me,' Charmian said, trying hard to keep the tremble from her voice, though her legs felt as if they would give way at any moment, 'my husband—will—will kill you for sure.'

'Husband? You still expect me to believe that, do you?' He made a lunge towards her but she dodged backwards. De Lisle licked his lips. Her rebuff only heightened his desire. He came forward again. This time he had her pinioned in a corner. There was nowhere else for her to escape. He grasped her shoulders and pulled her towards him pressing his wet mouth on her lips, forcing his tongue between her teeth, while his hand gripped her dress and made as if to tear it from her.

With a viciousness born of desperation, Charmian bit down hard upon his probing tongue. With a cry of pain he released her and stepped back. She saw the fury on his face, knew that she had enraged him as he raised his hand to strike her. But then her fear poured strength into her body. She lunged herself at him pushing him backwards. The unexpectedness of her attack caught him off balance and he reeled backwards, falling heavily and knocking his head against the corner of the table. As he went down she heard him give a deep groan.

Charmian lingered to see no more. Wrenching open the doors, she fled from the house, leaving her cloak behind. Picking up her skirts, she ran, half-sobbing, along the street, distraught, dishevelled and completely lost. Only when breathlessness caused her to slow, did she stop and look about her. She had run into a street bustling with life, but no one took any notice of her. The overhanging buildings made the street dark and the stench from the open sewer made Charmian feel a little ill.

Timidly she entered a baker's shop where even the appetizing aroma of freshly baked bread could not allay the street smells.

'Please—could you tell me the way to the Palace of Whitehall?'

'Why, certainly, miss.' And the baker, his apron covered with flour, took her out on to the street and gave her clear directions. ' 'Tis a long walk, miss,' he added looking down at her.

She smiled faintly. 'I shall find it. Thank you for your kindness.'

At the moment when Charmian was leaving the baker standing watching her walk up the narrow street, Campbell was striding through the Palace of Whitehall. Everywhere were Royalist Cavaliers, standing together in groups talking and laughing.

'Master Campbell, Master Campbell Denholm.'

Campbell turned to see a breathless and mud-bespattered groom from Ashleigh Manor hurrying towards him. At once Campbell knew that Jem's sudden arrival meant that something was wrong at Ashleigh Manor.

'What is it, man? My father?'

The groom paused to catch his breath and shook his head. 'Nay, he follows on and will be here 'ere long, young master. Nay, 'tis your wife. She has been missing from the Manor since early morning. We—your father feared she had set out for London and we have heard at an inn along the way that there was a young lady with three Royalists—one of them, de Lisle.'

On hearing this Campbell Denholm echoed the very same words his father had used only hours earlier when hearing the same news, 'My God—de Lisle!'

At once he turned to face the group of Royalists. Arms akimbo, he stood, a fearsome figure in his flowing cloak, and bellowed out, his voice ringing through the great hall for all to hear.

'Where is de Lisle?'

All eyes turned to look at him and all chatter and laughter ceased. Campbell scanned the faces for sight of someone—anyone—he knew was connected with the man he sought. He thrust a finger forward. 'You, Radcliffe, you are his friend. Where is he?'

'I—I—er—we've just left him at his town house.'

Campbell walked slowly towards Radcliffe, who took a nervous step backwards. 'Had he,' Campbell asked menacingly, 'anyone with him?'

Radcliffe gave a nervous laugh and looked about him for support. 'Only a wench we picked up on the road. A Puritan wench running away ...'

Campbell's hand was at his throat. 'That wench is my *wife!*' he roared and lifted Radcliffe from the floor. 'If harm has come to her, Radcliffe, you'll not live to see another dawn, nor de Lisle along with you.'

'We did her no harm, Denholm, I swear it. But now, well, de Lisle has her. We—we did not believe her when she said she was your wife.'

Campbell let him drop to the floor again the man fingered the bruise on his throat. 'She told you who she was?'

'Oh yes, but we thought it a ploy to secure her escape.'

Grimly Campbell strode away out of the hall, shaking his clenched fist in the air. 'Be warned, Radcliffe, if harm has come to her, I'll come looking for you.'

Charmian was winding her way through the strange streets trying to follow the baker's direction, whilst Campbell was galloping madly towards the house she had so recently left. Pedestrians scattered in all directions to avoid the flying hooves of his horse.

The front door was still standing open and Campbell ran up the steps three at a time and into the house. 'De Lisle! *De Lisle!*' Campbell bellowed and drew his sword. The house was quiet. Campbell glanced up the stairs and swallowed. He prayed he was not too late, for he would surely kill de Lisle if . . .

A groan came from the room on his right and entering, Campbell saw Anthony de Lisle trying to pull himself up from the floor. Blood poured from a wound on the back of his head where he had struck it on the sharp corner of the table. 'Oh my God!' he moaned as he looked up and saw Campbell standing over him, the point of his sword inches from de Lisle's throat. 'Then she was telling the truth.'

'Indeed she was,' Campbell said grimly. He saw her cloak lying on a chair nearby and the fear swept through him afresh. 'Where is she, de Lisle? If you have harmed her, I shall kill you, I swear it.'

'I have not hurt her, Denholm,' de Lisle looked up from where he still sprawled on the floor. Though I'll admit I tried to seduce her. I have never been one to shirk the truth. Whatever else my faults are, I am not lying to you. I brought her here. I didn't believe her tale about being married to you.'

'So I understand from your friend Radcliffe. But where is she now?'

'I really do not know. She fought me like a wildcat. God, Denholm, you've got yourself a fiery piece there and no mistake!'

Campbell could not prevent the surprise from showing on his face. Charmian—his Charmian—fighting like a wildcat?

De Lisle touched the back of his head gingerly. 'I suppose she's run off. She was trying to get to the Palace of Whitehall.'

'Damnation!' Campbell muttered. 'I've just come from there.'

He sheathed his sword and grinned suddenly amused by the picture of Charmian fighting this man. What courage!

'Well, de Lisle. I'll believe you. Scoundrel though you are, I know you to be a man of your word. Here, my hand,' and Campbell helped the man to his feet where he stood swaying unsteadily. 'I'll be on my way to find her.'

Slowly now, Campbell rode through the streets on his way back to the Palace of Whitehall searching for the slight figure of his wife. He was thoughtful now, seeing his young bride in a new light. He had thought her a child still, a petulant rather foolish child, but now he began to see things more from her point of view.

She had fought de Lisle's unwelcome advances, but she had not fought Campbell on their wedding night. A small smile quirked the corner of his mouth at the remembrance of that night, even amidst his anxiety about her. The thought gave him hope. Her show of resistance at the marriage ceremony had only been a token one. He had thought her weak, but now he began to see that she possessed a strength of will that he had not understood.

Hope began to surge in his heart. Did this mean that in spite of her reluctance to admit it, she did love him? He had loved her for so long Campbell thought, ever since they had first met when she had been a child. All through his years of exile the thought of her had been sharp in his memory. But bitterness had clouded his mind, for he knew she was betrothed to another and that she could never be his—not whilst Cromwell ruled. He had feared that, even if he was ever able to return to England, by that time she would be married to Joshua Mason. Then, on their return from exile, to meet her again—grown into a beautiful woman—to hear that she was not yet married, hope and longing and love had stirred. But her refusal to treat him as anything but an enemy had angered and embittered his tempestuous pride. And so he had treated her cruelly, yet all the time hating himself for doing so.

He remembered her words, 'I did not want to spend my life with a man who despised me.'

Was that what she thought of his feelings for her? He considered his behaviour to her of late and, chagrined, he realized it had not been like that of a lover. The years of exile, the ill-treatment he and his father had suffered, their anxiety about Lady Denholm in England during their enforced absence, all had combined to drive Campbell and Charmian further apart. On his return, he had not been able to reach out to the child he had loved, who was now a lovely woman, and he had blamed her for being caught up in something she had been powerless against—the power of her own father over her. And yet he had loved her still.

All the while he rode through the streets of London searching for her, his mind wrestled to try to understand her feelings, her beliefs. He could not now question her courage—even if he did not agree with her motives—in coming to London, alone, to try to save the lives of her father and friends for would not he have done the same if the circumstances had been reversed? It was an action that deserved his admiration. For even after her father's cruelty and abuse, she could not deny filial duty. She could not sit idly by and let her father perish.

There was only one fear left now in Campbell's heart that Charmian loved Timothy Deane, and that that love had driven her to take such a desperate action.

He reached the Palace once more and entered and then stopped in amazement. There in the centre of a circle of Royalists stood the tiny, resolute figure of his wife. Her plain grey gown was spattered with mud, her golden hair curled untidily from the prim Puritan bonnet she still wore, but she held their attention. They were paying her the courtesy of listening to her. Unseen, he tiptoed nearer.

'... your King—our King, for I am now the wife of a Royalist and proud to be—has already said that he wants no more bloodshed, other than the full penalty from those directly concerned with his own father's death. But even for them, he will want a fair trial. He would not thank you for putting men to death in his name but without his consent.' Her eyes glowed with a fire. 'It could cause another civil war—you could turn the people against you yet again, where as now, let me tell you, the common people are ready to welcome back their King with open arms.'

There was a murmur amongst the assembly and Campbell pushed his way through the circle around her.

'Charmian,' he said softly. She turned to face him, the surprise on her face giving way to joy and relief—and love. He opened his arms to her and she ran into them with a cry of thankfulness and was enfolded in his strong embrace.

The Cavaliers, smilingly, melted into the shadows.

'Oh my love, my love.' He stroked her hair and covered her face with kisses. 'You are not hurt? Say you are not harmed?'

'Oh Campbell—I am not hurt. And pray will you forgive me?'

'I understand, my dearest dear.' He looked down at her solemnly, cupping her beloved face in his hands.

'Did you follow me to London? Did you guess what I had done? Oh but I am so glad to see you,' she added and buried her head against him, clinging to him.

'Follow you? No—I was here first.' Now it was Campbell's turn to admit deception. 'When Wentworth brought the news I set out straight away for the city to try to prevent my Royalist brothers from taking action before the King's return, but I left word that you were not to be told.'

'Why? I believed you did not care whether my father and the Deanes lived or died.'

Wistfully, Campbell smiled. 'My darling, I am an impetuous, proud fool—and jealous too.'

'Jealous? I do not understand.'

Soberly he said, 'I—I thought your anxiety for the prisoners was because you were in love with Timothy Deane.'

Charmian shook her head, remembering so vividly the way they had parted. 'How could you ever think that of me? I liked him, yes, he was kind to me, but I fell in love many years ago with a young man who showed me laughter and joy,' her cheeks were pink as she professed her love for him. 'Then I lost him to the

Royalist cause. Where did he go during those years of exile, Campbell? Why did the gentle, laughing young man change so?'

'He is still there underneath, Charmian,' Campbell whispered, caressing her cheek with the tip of his finger. 'You shall help me to find him again, my princess.'

On the 30 May, 1651, King Charles the Second rode in triumph through the streets of London, lined with wildly cheering crowds.

It was several days before Campbell Denholm was able to bring his prisoners before the King for there was so much for His Majesty to do and so many petitioners to receive.

'My love, I must tell you,' Campbell told Charmian as he led her into the ante-room where they were to wait for audience with the King. 'Since you saw him, your father is much changed. He has been ill and is palsied.'

Though Campbell had given her this warning, Charmian was still shocked by the sight of her father. He was a shrunken, pathetic figure. His head lolled to one side, and he could not seem to speak properly. His left arm hung loosely by his side and when he walked he dragged his left foot. As they followed the prisoners into the room where the King received them, Charmian whispered, 'Oh Campbell, my father scarcely looks the same man.' Rising from her curtsy, Charmian looked with curiosity at the young man who was now her King. The long brown hair curling to his shoulders, the tiny line of moustache upon his upper lip. He was indeed a fine-looking man. Campbell was speaking, his deep voice ringing through the huge room. 'Your Majesty. You see before you three traitors. But—my wife and I—we come to plead mercy for them. Two of them were involved in the plot against your father, but as you can see, Joseph Radley has suffered a grievous illness since his arrest. He can be of no more danger to you. Sire, and as he is my wife's father . . .' Campbell smiled and leaned towards the King as if knowing His Majesty would appreciate the irony of the situation. 'It was not his wish that his daughter should marry a Royalist, you understand.'

The King smiled. 'Is this your wife?' he asked looking into

Charmian's face. Again she curtsied deeply. The King regarded her for a moment, then his smile broadened. 'I think Fate has decreed a just penalty upon Joseph Radley. I will demand no further punishment. What about the other two with him, Denholm?'

But before Campbell could reply, Charmian stepped forward impulsively and knelt upon the steps leading up to the chair where the King sat.

'Your Royal Majesty—I know all three have done you a great wrong and should be punished, but I beg you to spare Timothy Deane. He was kind to me when I most needed protection and I believe his only fault has been to be misled by his elder brother.' She glanced at the frightened face of the young boy. 'I am sure, Sire, given the opportunity he would serve you loyally now.'

'And the elder Deane?' the King asked, amused by Charmian's boldness, but certainly not angered by it.

Charmian hesitated and glanced at the sullen, obstinate face of William Deane. He would not swear allegiance to the King, she knew. She took a deep breath and met the King's eyes with a direct and honest gaze. 'Sire, I know you feel that enough blood has been shed—too much. May I humbly beseech you to spare his life? Perhaps—exile?'

The King eyed Charmian shrewdly. 'My young friend.' He spoke to Campbell, yet his gaze was upon Charmian. You have found yourself a remarkable bride. I congratulate you.' He smiled again. 'I cannot resist such a pretty plea. It shall be as you say. But mark you, William Deane,' he said, turning towards his onetime enemy, all good humour gone in a second. Now there was steel in the King's tone. 'Mark you well, if I ever hear that you have set foot on English soil again, it will be to certain death.'

Together Campbell and Charmian left the Palace of Whitehall and entered the coach which would take them back to Ashleigh Manor to begin their life together.

'I cannot change overnight, my darling,' Campbell told her soberly. 'I shall lose my temper often and . . .'

'Oh,' said his wife snuggling happily against him. 'I am beginning to find that I quite enjoy a challenge.'

Campbell laughed and drew her closer. 'As long as you promise never to knock me down and wound me as you did poor de Lisle.'

'Poor de Lisle indeed!' Charmian retorted hotly. 'He would have—have . . .'

'Yes, I know,' murmured Campbell tracing his finger round the outline of her face. 'And if he had succeeded with his wicked intention, then I would have killed him.'

'Would you—would you really?' Charmian asked.

'Indeed I would,' Campbell answered and silenced any more of her questions with his lips.

Lightning Source UK Ltd.
Milton Keynes UK
UKHW03f0216230418
321482UK00001B/45/P